THE WAR OF ART

THE WAR OF ART

Philip Blackpeat

iUniverse, Inc.

New York Lincoln Shanghai

The War of Art

Copyright © 2005

iUniverse books may be ordered through booksellers or by contacting:

iUniverse
2021 Pine Lake Road, Suite 100
Lincoln, NE 68512
www.iuniverse.com
1-800-Authors (1-800-288-4677)

ISBN-13: 978-0-595-36372-8 (pbk)
ISBN-13: 978-0-595-67372-8 (cloth)
ISBN-13: 978-0-595-80809-0 (ebk)
ISBN-10: 0-595-36372-5 (pbk)
ISBN-10: 0-595-67372-4 (cloth)
ISBN-10: 0-595-80809-3 (ebk)

Printed in the United States of America

To Artemis
To Filippos and Terpsichori
To Andy and Eliza
Το γιαγιά

CHAPTER 1

▼

"If art were revolutionary, the police would stop it." These were the words of a twentieth-century Greek painter, better known for his wit than for his portraits of sailors. He was answering a rather breathless comment made by a young man about a "revolutionary" painting. Greeks, my compatriots, tend to enshrine their noted artists of the day as "sacred monsters." That reverence often extends to unexamined acceptance of their pronouncements. Perhaps this was why I had always regarded this put-down as apt. I was reminded of it, for example, every time one of my Washington law firm partners would speak of a "radical" solution to a legal problem. On the morning of Friday, November 7, 2003, I did not know that the events about to unfold over the next few days would call into serious question the smug aphorism of the sailor portraitist.

Certainly, the roomful of late-period Picassos surrounding me on that morning did not appear any more revolutionary than a photo spread from the pages of *Architectural Digest*. I did not know much about these matters. It seemed to me, however, that "cutting-edge" art always saw its edge blunted soon after brandishing it. The process appeared to unfold in three stages. First, shock; second, bargaining (with the "visionary" art dealer); third, embrace. It somewhat resembled three of the stages of the death process laid down by Dr. Elisabeth Kübler-Ross: denial, negotiation, and acceptance. Take a shark, presumably having completed its own death process. Put it carefully in formaldehyde. Then wait for a rich man or woman to "collect" it. This seemed to be a good parable for the place of art in the western world.

For Pablo Ruiz Picasso, of course, the process had long run its course. His art had become the perpetual new black—fashionable yet accepted. Knee-jerk skeptics of modern art might still scoff at seeing everyday objects discombobulated on his canvases. They might be amused at seeing frontal eyes on his profiles and features strewn all over his faces. They might be perplexed by his chameleonic change of styles from one period to the next. But the Picasso canon had long ceased to shock.

And the age of bargains was also gone. Some day, there may surely be a Picasso recession in the art market. In the thirty years since the master's death, however, prices for his work have been going nowhere but up. It has been a bull market as vigorous as one of his *toros*. In 2003, one of my knowledgeable colleagues had informed me, there were very few things available for private ownership that cost more than a blue period Picasso. These early works were in turn among the few things more expensive than an early cubist oil painting. And even prices for late-period Picassos had reached a stratosphere to which initially people had not thought they belonged. The mark of a great artist, justly prized? Yes. The mark of wealth and taste? Yes and perhaps. But revolutionary? No, of course not.

Such were the thoughts I had while waiting in the Picasso room for Mr. X, a man of notorious wealth and unknown taste. Mr. X was the owner of the pictures. He also owned the room, the house in rural Maryland to which I had spent two hours driving that morning, and presumably much else. In addition, Mr. X was my new client, a fact that elated as well as mystified me. Washington lawyers like me specialize in representing large companies, not individuals. We undertake hypertechnical matters before a number of federal government agencies—matters of painstaking research and dry writing. The particular agency that I specialized in was the FOC, or Federal Oil Commission. It was an organization with no relationship to the arts whatsoever, unless one counts the corporate collections of large oil companies.

So I was surprised when Mr. X had called me the day before. As he had explained, he wished to retain my services on what he called a matter of provenance for a newly acquired piece of his collection. Law firms are good at creating in their lawyers a Pavlovian association between saying no to a client and acute physical pain. I therefore found it easy to suppress any inclination to tell Mr. X plainly that I was not an expert in provenance law, if this was indeed the field in which he required my services. Nor, of course, was I a private investigator or any other type of fact hunter or gatherer.

Facts are somewhat looked down upon in Washington, certainly in the legal community. I do not mean that in the spirit of anti-Washington cynicism. I mean it in the spirit of the French dictum: "it may work in practice, but does it work in theory?" Many in Washington find facts less interesting than the theory in which they might fit. Graduates of prestigious French schools of administration apparently share this view. Centers of bureaucratic machinery all over the world are less different from each other than people might imagine. They all disdain practicality. In this era of strained relations between the U.S. and France, a recognition of this common trait shared by the two capitals might help bring our two nations closer.

While I refrained from articulating my surprise, I still entertained qualms about this new representation. I did not even know whether questions of provenance were covered by my firm's legal malpractice insurance. Indeed, I didn't know whether one could even commit malpractice in such an area. On that latter question, I soon comforted myself. "Screw-up" and its variants are among the most commonly used expressions in Washington, whatever the area of your endeavor. That is why professionals in Washington have the ingrained instinct of rushing to blame someone else.

On the phone, Mr. X displayed the impatience with explanation that sometimes accompanies great wealth. So I was not given the opportunity to ask any questions anyway. "To understand what I want you to do and why I want you to do it," he said, "you must see the picture." He explained that he wanted this matter resolved within ten days, and that therefore my visit should take place immediately. The apparent arbitrariness of the deadline helped make me feel at home. Respect for inexplicable urgency is another hallmark of the Washington legal practice.

So there I was, waiting for Mr. X. On my way up the winding driveway that cut across X's estate, I had been unable to see the house until I practically bumped into it. Although predictably vast, it was all on one floor. More than its size, its lack of a vertical dimension flaunted the fact that a man of X's resources was unfettered by shortages of space. Architecturally, it was fifties modernist. Exposed concrete, painted white, was the predominant building material.

The style could only be described as austere. For all the technical labels, it seems to me that the modernist style of architecture comprises basically two schools. One is "form follows function." The other is "form looks good appearing to be functional." X's house belonged squarely to the purist, first school. It displayed none of the aerodynamic lines that more swashbuckling modern architects know how to mask as functional. There were no dramatic projecting planes and no plays of the light on seemingly accidental irregularities of the concrete surface. Just the clean volumes of a box. Not that this pure approach was truly functional either. It was a temple of worship to the idea of function, rather than the real thing. The only true utility of a twenty thousand square foot house is to house a rich man.

One of X's men had opened the door. The interior, too, was sparsely contemporary. Vast spaces receded into the distance. You knew they were not infinite, but nor did they seem finite. The rooms were not over-decorated. They could hardly be since I couldn't spot any utilitarian furnishings from my vantage point in the entrance. The bareness did not seem studied. It did not radiate the just-so perfection that decorators are paid to conjure up. In fact, the house appeared almost drab. But even its drabness suggested money and power. My host did not need to strive too hard for a uniform sense of high style.

He did not need to, but not because of modesty. The story was told eloquently by his wealth's dumb witnesses—the art hanging from the walls, suspended from the ceiling, and protruding from the floor. The brisk pace of my escort, and my nervous apprehension at meeting my client, produced a blur that prevented me from taking in the exhibits with much specificity. My peripheral vision was enough to confirm I was in the presence of several iconic works of pioneering boldness. But I could not quite tell what they were icons of.

The edge of my eye did register two patrolling policemen. I didn't have time to check whether they were in motion. I could, nevertheless, infer that they were a hyper-realist sculpture based on the sheer incongruity of a police patrol in a tycoon's house. Albeit in effigy, the officers created a forbidding impression. They loomed as symbolic, fully paid-for guards of X's property—the state at X's service. A balloon-shaped dog exhibited nearby was rather less formidable: it resembled Snoopy more than Cerberus. But there were no cartoonish sculptures in the windowless room to which my escort finally led me. Just the Picassos and the spotlights pointed at them.

For me, art collectors had always been creatures of mystery for a simple reason: the magic anonymity of the words "private collection" that accompany the public display of many privately owned works. The sight of those words next to a museum exhibit had often set off in my mind a vaguely pleasant line of inquiry about who these people were. One could only divine what worlds of uncommon refinement they must inhabit. So, I fully expected that piercing the veil of anonymity and actually meeting a collector of Mr. X's stature could result in disappointment.

In that expectation, at least, I was not disappointed. Mr. X was a short and balding man of about fifty. He would have been a rather common-looking man, but for a large bulbous nose, a shade more purple than the rest of his face, which served as an unusually comfortable seat for thick tortoiseshell glasses. The unnatural nose made him look like a retired clown, a fact that his entourage must have seldom discussed with him. The small eyes behind the glasses were as serious as a clown's usually are, but not melancholy.

As to his dress and accessorizing, I couldn't help noticing a number of *faux pas*. He wore his corduroy trousers with sneakers, a sweater was tucked in the trousers, and a hefty ring shone on the middle finger of his left hand. These sartorial choices immediately brought him down in my mind from the Valhalla of anonymous demigods to twenty-first-century, fashion-challenged America. The tucked in sweater and the corduroy-sneaker combination? Capital fashion offenses in the Greece of my youth. But to do justice to Mr. X—and to America—these things do change. The ring? I have never been able to understand many American men's infatuation with those trinkets, vaguely associated with educational or military institutions. Perhaps the cause is an unconscious yearning for a more stratified class system than American meritocracy, for a sense of unearned belonging.

Not that Mr. X had been born or bred in the American system. His faintly Germanic accent was hard to trace because of a rapid fire delivery that barely gave the listener time to register it. It reminded me, nevertheless, of the vague biographical accounts I had read on the Web the night before. According to these reports, he had immigrated from an unidentified Central European country several decades ago. He had done so for tantalizingly unexplained reasons. He must have been in his twenties at the time—no year of birth was publicly available either. His fast, and vast, enrichment was, of course, American enough to make up for his obscure foreign origins. His appeared to be the classic rags to riches story. The rags were separated from the riches by a period of questionable, but not demonstrably illegal, endeavor. Whatever questions had been raised by Mr. X's aggressive moneymaking activities thirty or forty years back, they had not survived the success of these activities. No blot had been left on his current reputation as an art-loving philanthropist. Men of means with an interesting past have the means to make it less interesting.

Truth be told, the Google research I had undertaken about Mr. X also suggested that he had not yet made it to the Mount Olympus of the super-collectors. He was not one of the handful of men who could afford to go, always and only, for the best. As my knowledgeable colleague at the office had explained to me, "best" in this context meant not the best artistically, but rather the hardest to get. If Vermeer had painted another three hundred masterpieces even more exquisite than the thirty-some in existence, the laws of the market would have overridden the laws of aesthetics. The extra supply of the works would have depressed their prices, quality notwithstanding. As it is, acquiring one of the extant Vermeers is one of the most difficult things in the world. And it is harder still to get one of unimpeachable authenticity. Eighty of the thirty-two known Vermeers are found in America, had quipped Orson Welles, another sacred monster with a gift for wit. It is likewise a Herculean feat to own one of the four or five first-class Van Gogh portraits still in private hands. Ditto, one of the Warhol "Shot Red Marilyn" silk screens. The reason is that they had the unlikely good fortune to be shot through by a lunatic, adding millions to their value. For any of these things to be yours, it is not enough to be able to cut a check for an astronomical amount. You also have to find a seller for whom that number makes any difference. Such are the achievements by which these men measure up against one another in a fierce ego contest.

Not that art collecting can fairly be characterized as a phallic competition. Women are better represented in the ranks of art collectors than in those of air pilots or chefs. Collecting seems to produce a unisex sort of ego rush. The reason? "Investing" in properties that do not bear any income and do not have any use is the best proof possible that one has satiated all one's needs. This also points to another necessary condition of the über-collectors' mindset. They never buy to resell. According to my knowledgeable colleague, some rich modern collectors have become richer still by resorting to a simple trick. They buy an artist en masse, thereby giving him prominence, and then happily flip his work. The true Olympians of art acquisition would never stoop to such practices. Trading is needy, and they have no time for need. They buy to possess.

In any event, X was not in what would be called the same "league" by sportswriters and, increasingly, political columnists. Apparently, his first art dealings dated from the time when he was still in the business of shading his reputation, before he had set out so successfully on the reverse job of whitewashing it. According to Google, he had dabbled in some German and Austrian expressionist works decades ago. His role in those transactions was murky. Was he a principal? A middleman? Both? Such as it was, that role had resulted in a messy legal battle over an Egon Schiele painting. I had even found some reported court opinions from the case, *Klein v. X*. The tangled dispute involved the work's prior chain of ownership. The case was ultimately dismissed when a previous owner of the work, an unidentified American heiress, had testified on X's behalf.

Cleared of any wrongdoing, X had started his collection in earnest a few years later. By that time, he had shifted his choice of style entirely. He became a kind of Maecenas for contemporary artists. He particularly favored those pioneers who could claim the most provocative pedigree. Their reputation was often earned by using various methods of embalming dead animals, and letting live ones loose in gallery spaces. Their common goal was to incite the question "but is it art?" in the minds of the art world, ever ready to be shocked as if for the first time. According to Kipling, the question had first been asked by no less an art connoisseur than Satan, when Adam produced the first drawing. It had since graced the lips of many comparatively less sinister experts. But, unlike Lucifer, they were no longer asking "it's pretty, but is it art?" The art world had long exorcised prettiness. It had done so with fervor greater than that of a stigmatic who abjures the first art critic himself.

After years of collecting in relative obscurity, X had gained his first notoriety in the early nineties. The reason was the destruction of a work he owned in circumstances whose freakishness came to be viewed as emblematic of the extremes of contemporary art. The work in question was a sandbox. Its sand was arranged to depict the flags of all the countries in the world. It was populated by a colony of ants that gradually eroded the flag shapes by moving the sand around. While the work was on loan to an art fair, the ants met an untimely death when formaldehyde leaked from a nearby exhibit showcasing the corpse of a cow. Litigation had ensued (again) when the insurance company had balked at paying a large amount of money for what it viewed is a minor—and replenishable—disruption of the ecological balance. It was quickly settled, however. An array of art experts hired by X had attested to the consensus of the art world that the particular ant colony had been unique to the artist's vision.

Soon thereafter, X had proceeded to "deepen" his collection with more respectable fare—late-period Picassos. The last period of the artist's life had long been dismissed by impressionist and modern art collectors as too radical. Of late, however, it had been embraced by avant-garde buyers for precisely the opposite reason—as a comparative nod to tradition.

But the fact that X had not reached the summit of art collecting made him no less remote or formidable from my vantage point. He was clearly mounting the final ascent. And likewise, the commonness of his appearance was not a sufficient justification to bring him down from his semi-Olympian heights. In fact, I remembered reading somewhere that world-class collectors tended to be unusually short and afflicted by a number of unattractive traits, for which their possessions were presumably intended as compensation. Large or deformed noses were one of those traits. They were common to titans such as J.P. Morgan, Peggy Guggenheim and Calouste Gulbenkian.

But I was not there to inspect Mr. X. I was there to inspect his latest acquisition. He briskly pointed me to the picture, hanging between two "sculptor and his model" drawings in front of us. It was an oil portrait of an androgynous, double-profile face. Man on the left, woman on the right. The artist had used light blue and gray hues for the distorted facial features, black for the disproportionate eyes and hair, and a solid orange for the backdrop. The canvas was square, about thirty by thirty inches. It was signed Picasso on the upper left. It bore an inscription in French, *La Clepsydre*, below the signature. Immediately underneath, a date had been inscribed: 26/7/37.

My first reaction was a wish I could afford it. The blurring of lines between art and commerce in unique art works frequently has that effect. In the mind of the viewer, aesthetic appreciation and the notion of a dollar amount become inseparable. Soon the former is expressed automatically in terms of the latter. I suppose that art dealers can be excused for having this unfortunate reflex. The fact that it has spread from the trade to the lay viewer must be a measure of the success of the art market's propaganda. Artists have helped by indulging the addiction themselves. Dali's delusional diaries report that he once paid for a restaurant meal with a quick drawing on the tablecloth and got back an "inferior" Picasso drawing as change. More likely than not, it was a faithful rendering of his signature that he had drawn.

Good manners, of course, required me to translate this initial reaction into a more socially acceptable form of appreciation. I had to pay Mr. X a compliment on his possession wholly apart from the capital he had had to expend to possess it. I was in the process of trying to find something nice to say, but it became immediately obvious that Mr. X had no interest in my aesthetic views anyway. "Now please come to my office," he said, in the rapid-fire staccato to which I was getting accustomed, "we will go through the facts." Ah, the facts. My experience had taught me that this is a more subjective term than it sounds.

CHAPTER 2

▼

X's office had the antiseptic look of a work space whose occupant does not write anything except his signature for a living. His desk was bare except for one slim stack of files near one corner. Lawyers aspire to such paperlessness, but only the most compulsive ever come close to it. It is the usual kind of human longing for the particular thing that is least within the grasp of each of us. But my envy for X's freedom from clutter was immediately tempered when I noticed a number of baseball caps lying on a shelf. Another blow at my perception of art collectors as superior beings. Would this man collect anything?

X pulled a manila folder from the stack and laid it open on his desk. From my chair, I could make out with some difficulty the words handwritten on the label: "Re Amore." Bizarre. Perhaps a recycled folder that used to house file information about an amorous entanglement of Mr. X's. Mr. X seemed to be a man of records.

I also remembered from my Google research that he was a man of many, and public, amorous entanglements. Collectors like to collect. "Old masters and young mistresses," was the motto of Gulbenkian. X's taste, on the other hand, ran to a uniformly recent vintage, both for the paintings on his walls and for the women in his bed. His air of self-assurance probably served to parlay his unattractive looks and no longer verdant age from liabilities to assets in his courting technique. Huge reserves of power are the most likely reason why an older man rather disadvantaged by nature can afford to behave like a confident predator.

"I bought the picture," he started, "at the May Sotheby's auction in New York, for a large amount that is part of the auction's public records, but that need not concern you in your project. It was what auctioneers like to refer to as 'fresh to the market'—in my view a highly overrated component of a work's market value. I don't know why fifty or sixty years off the market should create any guarantee of respectability or distinction. I could never understand why it should result in a higher price than a frequently traded work with well-documented provenance. In any event, this picture was certainly fresh. In fact, it had never changed hands before at a public auction.

"On the other hand, it also suffered from two significant demerits—a lack of documentation and a gaping hole in its provenance. There was never any doubt about the authenticity of the signature. But the work has never been recorded in the Zervos 'catalogue raisonné' or any of its supplements. As for provenance, I have learned the following from inquiries that I have made and that I do not want you to replicate. The whereabouts of the work remained unknown for more than sixty years. It emerged in 2001 in the hands of something called North American Research and Technology. NART is apparently one of those Tysons Corner high tech companies whose executives view art collecting as an appropriate way to fulfill their fiduciary duties to their shareholders. It was NART that consigned it to the auction house.

"Finally, the picture's title added to the unknowns. 'La Clepsydre' means hourglass in French, but there is nothing in the portrait that accounts for this title. This is unusual. For all his distortions of reality, Picasso was well known for disdaining abstraction."

A couple of times during this explanation, I tried to mumble "ah-hah" to reassure X of my unwavering attention, though X did not appear in need of reassurance in this or any other respect. But I was growing increasingly mystified about the nature of the project that was being assigned to me. "So," I stammered when he paused, "is this what you would like me to find? The meaning of the hourglass? Because—"

"I know the meaning of the hourglass," he interrupted, annoyed at my interruption. "Here, have a look at this." He pulled a black and white photograph from the Re: Amore folder and handed it to me. "This was mailed to me anonymously last week."

It was a grainy picture of the artist, Pablo Picasso, standing in his customary dress of nothing but a pair of shorts. He had a cigar in his right hand and some sort of cookie in the left. He must have been in his late fifties when the photograph was taken. His lips were molded into the ironic half-smile that successful men can afford. His aggressively balding head and large, flat nose similarly projected the willfulness of self-confidence. But what distinguished his looks from those of the average captain of industry, other than the bohemian state of undress, were the eyes. They projected the same astoundingly piercing gaze seen in all of his known photographs.

It was only after I extricated my own eyes from the famous face, however, that I realized the relevance of the photo. Hanging on the wall behind Picasso, right above his left shoulder, was a portrait of the same androgynous double profile I had just seen—Mr. X's picture. With one difference: next to the man's side of the profile, to the right as one faced the painting, there was one more figure. It was the face and bust of a woman holding something in her hands.

"A variation on the same theme?" I ventured. "No," X said categorically. For the first time during our rather one-sided conversation, he was showing some animation. "This is it, this is my picture. My picture has been altered. I think the word is 'vandalized.'" It was clear that, in Mr. X's view, his purchase of the painting had retroactively converted this perceived act of vandalism from an assault on civilized culture as a whole into a personal offense. "Here," he continued, "look at this. I had the photo enlarged and retouched."

The enlargement revealed three things that I had missed at first sight. First, the woman's face was rendered in a manner strikingly different from the double profile to its left. No cubist distortion altered the woman's traits. Rather, the face—oval, pale, high cheekbones, black hair—was drawn with exquisite accuracy in Picasso's "classical" style. With one exception: her left eye had lost any resemblance to its accurately drawn dark companion. It had been dislocated from its socket and undergone a ninety degree turn. While it still centered on a token pupil dotted in black, it had become more akin to a stylized tear about to stream down her cheek.

No art expertise was necessary to recognize the reference. It had been baked into the consciousness of myself and millions of other twentieth-century babies. It was a *Guernica* eye/tear. In *Guernica*, Picasso's most overtly political work, the eyes of the desperate upturned faces have been rotated downwards by the master. The earth's gravity has seemingly uprooted them and turned them into tears. The reason for the lament is famous. The tears are being forever shed over the tragedy of the Basque city's bombing in 1937. By contrast, the reasons for the tear that the pale woman's eye had become in X's painting were completely unknowable from the context. I made a mental note: judging from the date on the portrait, the two works would appear to have been painted in the same year.

And, the third thing that I had missed: the woman was holding an hourglass in her joined hands. At least, one enigma was resolved: the title of the work. Everything else, including the nature of Mr. X's need for my services, remained wrapped in mystery.

"I wonder who the woman is," I said stupidly, hoping that this was not the question that Mr. X was planning to pose to me.

"I know who the woman is," X grunted. "Compliments of my correspondent. I received this two days ago." He handed me another two pages from the folder. The first page was a brief e-mail message in French from an untraceable "hot-mail" address. It read:

Mon cher Monsieur X:

En ésperant que vous trouverez l'article suivant renseignant, je vous prie d'accepter, Monsieur, l'assurance de mes salutations les plus distinguées.

Votre Petit Marcel

I was in the process of enlisting the service of my rusty French, when I realized a translation, presumably in Mr. X's hand, was helpfully scribbled underneath.

Dear Mr. X:

Hoping that you will find the following article informative, I request, Sir, that you accept the assurance of my most distinguished regards.

Your little Marcel

I knew the "most distinguished regards" part to be standard French epistolary formality. But it was slightly inconsistent with the informal, Anglo-Saxonic medium of a brief e-mail, as well as the presumed intimacy of "little Marcel." Could Mr. X count a Marcel as one of his friends? "Needless to say, I know of no Marcel, little or large," Mr. X offered, anticipating my question.

I turned to the attachment. It was a one-paragraph story from *Le Figaro*, dated February 2, 1995. It had been converted to a "pdf" file for e-mailing, and it too was translated in the margin. Or rather, it was not, strictly speaking, a story. It was an entry in the obituary column:

Ex-Equestrian Meets Death She Escaped 75 Years Ago

Andrée Duplessis, 96, passed away Thursday, of massive head injuries she sustained when she was kicked by a horse that she had stepped behind. The tragic accident occurred in a moment of apparent absent-mindedness at the public stables of the Bois de Boulogne. A noted equestrian in her youth, Ms. Duplessis had won several competitive events during the 1910s. Her career was cut short by a severe fall during a competition in 1920. Prior to her accident, she had also been an accomplished tennis player. Ms. Duplessis was not married, and she leaves no known survivors behind.

The notice was accompanied by a photograph of a smiling young woman in riding uniform holding a cup. It was obviously the young Ms. Duplessis enjoying one of her victories.

There was naturally nothing in the young girl's insouciant pose to forebode the terrible end recounted in the notice, and the contrast made the story sadder. In all their unscrupulous machinations to increase copy, there is one trick to which tabloid editors have not resorted. To my knowledge, no one has yet thought to accompany all obituary notices with a picture of the deceased emerging victorious from a game in his or her youth. The reason has nothing to do with decorum or decency—they certainly run more unseemly stories. But no one, not even the most powerful press baron, wants to tamper with the reader's fundamental self-preservation mechanisms. The brilliant smiles in these pictures display their owner's irrational confidence that he or she is thoroughly buffered from death. The buffer is the prospect of a long run playing more games and beating more odds. No tabloid reader, even the most morbid, wants to be reminded that this sunny confidence, which he has foolishly entertained himself, is bound to prove misplaced in the end.

But, more to the point, there was no doubt: the woman holding the cup in the *Figaro* photograph and the woman holding the hourglass in the 1937 painting were the same person. Framed by black hair escaping from her riding cap, her face was unusually emaciated for the time. Its oval contours contrasted with the angularity of her high, Tahitian-like cheekbones. These were so pronounced that they almost made the face look cubist in real life, obviating any need for Picasso to distort its lines in the portrait done a couple of decades later.

Her eyes were dark and penetrating, like Picasso's own. They half-joined the smiling mouth in relishing her victory. But they also appeared to betray characteristics that had little to do with smiling: a habit of cool assessment; a touch of detached ennui; and the barest trace of a sensual memory. The same look might be expected to register on the eyes of an unusually alluring and adventurous member of the British royal family on a charity visit. She graciously accepts the tributes paid her, but she would rather be somewhere else doing less reputable things, and she was at exactly such a place last night.

The chief differences between the photo and the portrait, of course, were those of state of mind. The smile had morphed into a sober expression, and one of the enigmatic eyes had been replaced by the large eye/tear. Whatever worldly preoccupation had distracted her in the photo, it had nothing to do with tragedy. The eyes in the photo may have been distracted, but they were not grieving. The explanation for the eye/tear would seem to lie in the woman's future, not her past. The great artist's hole-burning gaze seemed to be piercing into time, decades beyond his own death, to foretell Andrée Duplessis's end—not untimely, but tragic nevertheless. When you have reached the age of ninety-six, you're probably entitled to expect that you will not die of an accident. You have the right, therefore, to wear the mask of tragedy if that expectation is upset. It would certainly have been more fitting if it was the portrait accompanying the obituary rather than the photograph.

"So this is the information I have," Mr. X said, interrupting a train of thought that he was justifiably not interested in paying me to entertain. "And here is the bottom line. Someone did not want anyone else to know that Picasso painted the likeness of a Ms. Duplessis. I want to know why."

Great. Mr. X's explanation had now definitively confirmed my fears. This project lay far afield from any conceivable expertise that my legal training and practical experience could lay claim to. "May I ask," I asked feebly, "why you have chosen our firm for this project? I am sure that you appreciate better than I that some of its aspects would benefit from the assistance of a private investigator. And, as you know, I am an FOC practitioner—"

"Two reasons," he interrupted. "First, I am not asking you who did it, who vandalized my picture. I am asking you why. I think the who will flow from the why. And I believe the why in this case cannot be answered by checking people's garbage, or I would indeed have hired a private investigator. I think it requires hard, analytical research of the kind that your firm is known for. And I know that the answer, or the beginning of the answer, must be in the man's life. So start with it. It has been the subject of more books than almost any other artist's. Have one of your young associates read all of them for leads. I do not see how this is not a perfectly suitable task for a lawyer and a perfectly unsuitable one for some kind of detective. By the way, you may also be assisted in this endeavor by little Marcel. Something tells me that this is not his last missive. I have responded to his e-mail by instructing him that all further communications should be sent to you as my counsel. Except I would not bother initiating a dialogue if I were you. I have already tried. A waste of time.

"But there is a second reason why I chose you." Mr. X closed the folder, and it was at that point I realized that I had misread the label: not "Re Amore," but simply "Re Andrée." Evidently I had misread Mr. X, too, as more of an eccentric than he was. His penchant for cataloguing, which I assume all collectors of a certain type must share, was at least based on categories that made sense to people other than himself.

Now Mr. X picked another piece of paper from the stack and handed it to me. The format of the document was immediately familiar. It was an FOC news release from February 2003. It set forth the dissenting statement of the agency's head, the widely respected Chairman Lower, in a proceeding concerning oil companies. I was familiar with the proceeding, too. The chairman had been overruled by a majority of the Commission in a multi-billion-dollar dispute over the prices that refiners pay crude oil providers. No matter how important it may have been in my practice, the relevance of this dispute to the portrait of Ms. Duplessis was, needless to say, lost on me. Until I noticed a passage in the text, highlighted in yellow, doubtless by Mr. X. Chairman Lower was finding fault in the strongest terms with the majority's opinion. In his view, the majority was reckless in proposing rules that differed from state to state instead of a unified body of regulation. The disparaging epithet he used? "Picassoesque."

I looked up at Mr. X. For the first time in our interview, he was smiling. It was the "eureka" smile of a visionary who has discovered a connection where inferior intellects see nothing. The man whom I had just downgraded from mildly eccentric to merely methodical was revealing himself to be very possibly demented.

I had heard of the type of "tycoon-conspiracy nut." Howard Hughes was an early example. I had also read of a right-wing billionaire who had set out to prove that our former president, Bill Clinton, had been involved in a number of murders, abductions and other capital crimes.

Then there was also the matter of the surrounding ambience: 2003 was certainly a year of conspiracy suspicions in Washington. The capital was buzzing with rumors of real motives being disguised by ostensible ones. Why did we go to Iraq? Was it the weapons of destruction, mass or of less massive caliber? Or was it some other, more opaque motivation? What did the administration know about the terrorists' plans before September 11? As much as it said it knew—or more? I personally was skeptical of most of these suspicions. But the combination of this fertile atmosphere and great wealth may have bred a new type of super-conspiracy nut, of which Mr. X was a specimen.

"You probably think I'm crazy." Mr. X said. He was at least sane enough to recognize that. "But my instinct tells me that this statement by your esteemed FOC chairman is not entirely unrelated to the matter you will be investigating. Think about that."

And he abruptly ended our meeting, leaving me to my bewildered thoughts on my way back to Washington.

CHAPTER 3

▼

Junior lawyers at large law firms must pine for the lost time of summers past, when they were summer associates, clerking at the firm in between law school years. Then, their career was in front of them. Its days would be full of the trial hearings, "strategy" sessions, and client meetings their over-promising employers took them to. Its holidays would brim with the delights of suburban life, including an exceptionally harmonious spouse and a family-wide aptitude for all kinds of sport. Such are the aspirations that corporate America holds out to its recruits as the rewards of hard work. Now, having joined the firm, they discover that many years of boredom—research, legal memos, and boxes of documents to be read and classified—are the price. It is a price exacted in return for a prize that has suddenly become more elusive rather than more tangible.

I knew, therefore, that many of my young colleagues at the firm would jump at a project as unorthodox as the one Mr. X had assigned me. They would greet it as a welcome break from the dry work to which they had found themselves consigned.

I was right. Paul, the bright associate who was my first choice to staff the project, was excited by it for the same reasons that made me so leery of taking it on in the first place—its quirkiness. Or at least so he said, when I summoned him to my office immediately after my return from rural Maryland on Friday afternoon. The mark of a good associate is not only to accept ungrudgingly assignments from the firm partners, but also to accept them with a measure of enthusiasm. Plus, for fear that he might think I, too, was crazy, I did not tell Paul anything about the more bizarre of Mr. X's directions. I didn't disclose the strange suspicions to which his "instinct" pointed him and which he had also asked us to pursue.

Paul was a recent arrival to the U.S. from Austria. But the circumstances of his coming to the country had none of the obscurity that surrounded X's trip over the Atlantic decades before. The typical European émigré of our day is a different species of adventure seeker than those of previous generations. True, the newcomers are equally motivated by opportunity. But their travel plans are not driven by the factors that often accounted for the itineraries of men like X: poverty, persecution, or inconvenient run-ins with the local authorities. Paul was one of the army of young professionals who ride their academic credentials from their home countries for their one-way trip. Their education earns them entry-level jobs at America's investment banks, management consultancies, and law firms. These institutions share an endearing trait. When you knock on their door, they don't care where you come from, whom you know, and who sired you or gave you birth. If you have money, they will work for you. If you have smarts, they will hire you.

The origins, therefore, of these bright young men and women are often less humble than those of their swashbuckling predecessors. By the same token, however, their opportunities are more limited. The goal most likely within their reach is modest professional affluence. It is a far cry from the vast riches that have been brought to the Xes of this country by unschooled drive, street smarts and luck.

Like X, Paul, too, had a Germanic accent. His, in fact, was more pronounced. His exposure to German-language education had been longer than X's, and the attempts of his tongue around the long vowels and dropped syllables of American English had been more recent. But his accent had almost the reverse effect on his diction. X's accent provided a guttural back tempo to his high-speed delivery. Paul's speech, on the other hand, was more high-pitched, with a funny musical lilt. His voice would sometimes become shrill for emphasis, like a slightly grating violin crescendo in an atonal concert.

While Paul's background was more conventional and better-mapped than X's, there was still a certain air of romantic mystery about him. He spoke many languages and was well traveled—in fact, I think that he had been to high school in Argentina for a couple of years. His parents, of whom he seldom spoke, had instilled in him excellent manners and a phlegmatic tolerance for all the usual types of professional hardship. Unflappable, he had endured all-night wakes, demanding clients and, worst of all, patronizing partners. He never invoked his crushing workload to say no to a new project. He never protested when on a Friday afternoon a partner gave him an assignment that would keep him in the office for most of the weekend. He never presumed to inquire about the more diverting weekend plans of the partner who was dumping the assignment on him. He would always arrive punctually for meetings, walking with a characteristic limp due to an unknown affliction of his left foot. I had not heard him utter one word in anger. Only occasionally did I spot a flash of steely impatience in his eyes, but it just as quickly disappeared.

Despite his sang-froid, Paul's face appeared to be the field of a constant battle between two competing faces. His green eyes, French nose and finely honed mouth were so handsome as to border on the cherubic. I have read studies showing that good looks improve career chances. My personal experience, however, suggests that the legal profession has not fully absorbed these scientific conclusions. Successful lawyers represent a true democracy of miscellaneous looks. An attractive appearance inspires doubt about the willingness of its beneficiary to spend long hours reading law books, and can raise suspicions of dilettantism. The bar was more surprised when John-John Kennedy finally passed the New York bar exam than when he had initially failed.

Possibly conscious of these professional perils, Paul had deployed the stratagem of wearing round gold-rimmed glasses that gave him a reassuring bookish aspect. But there was little risk anyway. Any concern in that regard could have been dispelled by his other, warring face, or more precisely the shape of his face. It was very long and very angular. In fact, it ended in pointed edges in all directions—his chin, his ears, and the top of his head—giving it the look of a rhomboid parallelogram. The notorious nineteenth-century eugenist Cesare Lombroso might have classified this shape of face as one of his criminal human types. If so, Paul's intellect and temperament, combined with his face's better half, would have been enough to discredit the theory.

Paul's European origin brought some extra advantages to our project besides his prodigious work habits and analytical skills. For one thing, he had a good knowledge of French. I was sure he spoke that language as exotically to the French ear as his English sounded off-center to the American. It could nevertheless come in handy in the event of more communications from little Marcel. He also possessed a familiarity with modern art. I vaguely suspected that he came from a family with considerable amounts of money, art, and culture to match. Associates are at the bottom of a firm's lawyer hierarchy, but many of them are more cultured than some of the firm partners. Indeed, it is the cultured ones who most frequently fail to make partner.

First, we had to organize ourselves, deploy the rigorous analytical methods for which, in part, Mr. X had selected us. "*Cherchez la femme,*" say the French. Look for the woman; she is the key to every mystery, at least every mystery worth solving. In capitalist America, this injunction had been replaced rather predictably by another—"follow the money." Neither admonition seemed to be a sound guiding principle for the task at hand, however. Here, we already had found the woman. What we needed to look for was her relationship with the man who painted her portrait and with another person, man or woman, who did not want anyone to know that fact. As for money, the financial rewards that someone could hope to reap by the defacing of an expensive painting were unclear.

Start with the artist's life, Mr. X had said, and that seemed as practical a methodological principle as any. "So," I said to Paul, "start reading. Richardson, Gertrude Stein, Ariana Stassinopoulos—later reinventing herself as Huffington. They have all written biographies or reminiscences of Picasso, of varying length, quality, and reliability." "So have some of Picasso's women, no?" Paul countered, providing the first useful insight for our inquiry. But of course: Picasso was notoriously a man of countless women, a bit like one of the satyrs he liked to depict. Andrée's possible status as one of these women was a plausible key into the mystery.

"Perhaps the answer is simple," Paul ventured further. "This could be a case of a jealous lover or wife defacing the portrait of another woman. Femicide in effigy, or voodoo vandalism. Perhaps the French are right: we do need to look for a woman after all. *La femme vandale.*" Paul ended his point one octave higher than he had started it.

It was an interesting hypothesis, but ultimately it was too problematic an explanation. First of all, why would Picasso's wife or other woman enjoying the master's favors in 1937 be so jealous of Andrée? The timing didn't work, as Andrée's likeness in the portrait dated probably from the 1910s. Admittedly, that problem was not impossible to overcome—love knows no age, and perhaps, nor does jealousy. But then the voodoo motivation was even more questionable. If a possessive woman was indeed the defacer, the motive was likely to be more complex than pure spite, even if spite did play a part. In any event, I told Paul, let's first focus on Andrée and her place in the master's life. We will worry about the perpetrator (or-trix) next. As Mr. X had said, the who will flow from the why.

As I had explained to my new client in our introductory phone conversation, an unalterable engagement would take me out of town for the weekend. The silence at the other end of the line had suggested that Mr. X did not greet the news with unalloyed enthusiasm. I had therefore rushed to reassure him that one of my capable young colleagues would be "holding the fort" and "advancing the ball" on his project. Under pressure from clients, lawyers are often reduced to mixed metaphors. When I left the office on Friday evening, I was nevertheless confident that Paul would live up to my reassurances, capably serve our client, and honorably acquit the law firm.

CHAPTER 4

▼

When Paul reappeared in my office early Monday morning, he was visibly less excited than he had been on Friday. "I went through all name indices for all of the books about Picasso that the library could procure," he said. "No mention of Andrée Duplessis. Then I hit Nexis and a number of Web search engines. A search for Pablo and Andrée in the same story yielded no results whatsoever. I also searched for any references to Andrée Duplessis by herself. A number of sites came up but none appears to concern our Andrée. Finally, I checked the standard French reference sources. No entry for her name in *Larousse* or any other encyclopedia. Evidently, her riding victories were not enough to win her the posterity of an encyclopedic reference."

So it was not going to be easy. In this information age, all our magical means of finding information in oceans of raw data have brought a curse along with their blessings. They have increased the inscrutability of any mysteries that they cannot uncover, and they have further empowered those possessing them.

What next? "Check for Andrées," I told Paul. "The *Figaro* piece says Andrée had never married, but this was an obituary reporter writing under the press of a deadline. It's easy to overlook a marriage or two, in such a long life. Check any references to equestrians, horse riding, horses, in the indices. Then start reading the texts, but focus on accounts of Picasso's life during the first twenty years of the century. The age of the woman in the portrait suggests almost for sure that he had made her acquaintance back then."

"What if he never knew her at all? What if he was painting after a photograph, perhaps the same one that was used by the *Figaro*? Pablo often did that." The extent to which Paul had embraced the problem posed to him—another mark of a good associate—had resulted already in first-name familiarity with his subject. Perhaps he would soon start calling the master Pablito. Perhaps this is what Andrée used to call him.

"And why would he pick an old picture of an obscure equestrian to paint from?" I countered. "Whether he used a photograph or his probably photographic memory, he must have chosen his subject because he knew the woman." And then another thing occurred to me. Pablo had not only painted Andrée's portrait. He had also had his own photograph taken in front of it. Was it an accidental backdrop, a function of where the man happened to be standing at the time of the click? The posed setting suggested not. Pablo had picked the portrait as background for the photograph. Was he sending a message? And was he encoding it in signs that could only be deciphered posthumously?

Perhaps, then, the photograph too held a key. But the problem was that there was nothing suggestive in it. In fact, there was nothing featured in it other than the man and the portrait. Who knows, perhaps the symbolism was hidden in the cigar, or the cookie. But I had given Paul enough assignments for the day. I let him go back and hit the books.

I turned to my computer screen and went to the Drudge Report on the Web. More American casualties in Iraq, months after the beginning of American occupation of that country. The press had adopted the morbid practice of accompanying each new report of Americans being killed with a body count. The numbers came complete with a breakdown between two periods: so many dead, so many of them after the president had declared an end to major combat activities. The reason for both the habit and the fact that it went unquestioned was obvious. They sprang from the nation's obsession with games, and its related mania with sports statistics. In fact, the president's declaration that the war was over served as a natural breaking point. It was a convenient way to create two halves and make the coverage even more akin to the games TV viewers liked so much to watch.

And that was not the only example, of course. Ever since we had gone to war, our politicians and press alike kept describing it in the assorted language of sport or game: "home run"; "scrimmage"; "he must show his cards." I remembered too that one of our top generals had talked about watching a college basketball game on television, on one of the most difficult days of our invasion.

There was an irony to this, because I was sure that games had originally been created as a simulation for war. They were combat without death as the forfeit. Now war was becoming a copy of its own copy, a sport with death as the forfeit. It was a cruel reversal of roles for the doomed soldiers' mothers. They were going about the habitual chores of life, with a burden on their mind, but unsuspecting of the specifics, even as the pieces of shrapnel were tearing through their boy's body. One day after, when their life has been scarred forever, his death would be immortalized in the language of football anchormen and baseball statistics.

I was also sure that sports, like war, had been created by men. Throughout recorded history, women had been too preoccupied with their realities to bother with such ritualistic reenactments. Decades of feminism, women's leagues, and female tennis stars had barely made a dent. Sports banter remained one of the tools for excluding women from the kind of macho camaraderie that generates clients and business. I had watched many female lawyers uncomfortably straining to share the general enthusiasm for a quarterback's performance over lunch at a steak restaurant. My own lack of the encyclopedic sports knowledge possessed by my male partners made me sympathize with their attempts to gain recognition as the men's worthy interlocutors.

But Andrée Duplessis appeared to be different. She was a distinguished equestrian and tennis player in the France of the 1910s. It must have been very unusual for a young girl at the time. On the other hand, I remembered reading somewhere that riding is one of the only sports where men and women compete against one another in the same event. Come to think of it, tennis too shares that characteristic in part: mixed doubles. I wondered whether that was the case for the two sports in the early twentieth century. Had Andrée beaten men as well as women in the competition whose prize she was triumphantly holding in the picture from *Le Figaro*?

These idle thoughts brought me back to the problem I was being paid to resolve. I decided, however, that any hope at cracking it would have to await Paul's new searches, and turned to a brief that demanded my urgent attention.

Regrettably, through no fault of his, Paul's second foray was as fruitless as his first. "Nothing," he said when he returned to my office three hours later. "I must have now scoured through every detail of Pablo's life and work. I have read about his periods—blue, pink, analytical cubism, synthetic cubism, classicism. I am dizzy with all kinds of scholarly exegesis. I have read about his women, real or painted. Fernande, the demoiselles of Avignon, Olga, Marie-Therese, Dora, Françoise, Jacqueline. I have read about his male friends and their women. Andrée Duplessis, or anyone who might be her, simply does not register. I found horses, of course, many horses. The screaming horse in the central panel of *Guernica*, for example. It is apparently a symbol for the defeated people. But it is riderless."

Not good. This was becoming one of those projects for which the lawyer must compose a particularly challenging memorandum to the client. For all their focus on practical training, U.S. law school curricula don't adequately prepare lawyers for this delicate task. The memo must detail the exhaustive research the lawyer has undertaken, for which the client will promptly receive an invoice. It must then explain cogently why that research has, nevertheless, borne no results. Clients don't like such memos.

But we could not give up. Paul's listing of Picasso's different styles gave me an idea. Perhaps there was a clue to be found in the style he used in the 1937 portrait. Or, more accurately, in the jarringly dissonant styles. Why had Picasso done the man-woman profile in his cubist manner and the portrait of Andrée in the classical manner, with the exception of the eye? Was there something to be read in the contrast? I realized I was probably grasping at straws. But it was not as if there were any other promising avenues, indeed any other avenues, that we could follow.

A guy I knew, Christopher Nolan, was a free-lance columnist and author. His focus was the eclectic triptych of modern art, politics, and nightlife. What if I showed him the picture behind Pablo in the photograph? X had kindly provided me with an enlarged copy of the photo. But I had to get X's permission first. The photo was clearly a client confidence. As far as I knew, it had never been placed in the public domain.

So I sent X a quick e-mail: "OK to show the photograph of Picasso with the painting to an art writer I know, Christopher Nolan? Very knowledgeable. Might shed light on the style, etc." Mr. X replied in a matter of minutes: "OK to show Andrée's face. Face only."

The promptness of his response disquieted me somewhat, for reasons of self-preservation. Here was this busy and powerful man, assigning a high priority to a project that I had still made zero progress on. Plus, the constraint he imposed—face only—disposed of my hope to obtain some expert insight on the contrast in manner between the face and the double profile. But such were my instructions. I had my assistant make a truncated copy of the picture by means of some expert Xeroxing. It was, in a way, the reverse defacing from the destruction that the picture had already suffered. I then e-mailed the result to Nolan, asking him to kindly take a quick look at it and inviting him to lunch.

Unsurprisingly, he accepted despite the short notice. I knew Nolan to be particularly susceptible to the pleasures of the table. An Englishman and Cambridge graduate, Nolan possessed a great talent for self-aggrandizement, usually lubricated by alcohol. He also had an inexhaustible capability for contradicting everyone's views. That included views he had himself passionately defended when attacking someone else's point on the prior evening. I have often wondered about the genesis of this curious mind-set among a surprisingly large number of Oxbridge alumni. It may be the opposite phenomenon to Americans' infatuation with signet rings. It appears to spring from resentment at a class system that does not accord sufficient respect to these debating gladiators' merit, as perceived by themselves.

In Nolan's case, however, that perception was more or less deserved. His annoying self-importance disguised, instead of the intended effect of highlighting, the fact that he was a true polymath. He had vast and in-depth knowledge of a lot of things. In a sense, he combined the European humanist model of knowing a little about everything with the American specialist model of knowing everything about one thing. And the entire span of modern art was one of the areas to which he had applied himself.

Truth be told, I also did not mind a break from the kind of work that ties a lawyer to his desk. Sadly, meals that mix business and pleasure are one of American professionals' principal sources of pleasure. I told my secretary I was off to a quick lunch. She knew by now this meant an absence of at least two hours and a mild decrease in my afternoon productivity due to the modest consumption of alcohol. I gave her a typing project and headed out of the office.

CHAPTER 5

▼

The small Italian restaurant was dark, as if better to highlight its specialties—white truffles generously grated on pasta, whole fish flown from the Mediterranean. Nolan was already seated when I arrived. He was a short, stocky man. His head was big, and his long hair was rather too youthful for his forty-five years. His brow was covered by bangs. He would sometimes deploy them as a debating tool, throwing them back from his eyes with a leonine movement of the head when he wanted to emphasize either a point or his superiority. He wore a worn denim shirt and loose-fitting tweed jacket, whose donnish elbow patches were located over his elbows rather approximately. Incongruously, a red silk scarf was tucked inside the shirt, dandyish as well as outmoded.

Perhaps the style clash was an attempt to straddle the intellectual community to which he rightfully belonged and the more effete circles to which he had aspired. Sartorial choices are often fossilized versions of who we wanted to be decades ago. Or perhaps the Wildean flourish of the scarf had initially been intended as the sacrificial gesture of a heterosexual to a public school milieu where effeminacy was *de rigueur*. I remembered one of Nolan's scholarly pieces, entitled "*Onanism: the Artist's Elusive Orgasm.*" It had included a lengthy digression on the social cost of resisting a certain mutual courtesy that is apparently common in English boarding schools.

I had read the piece a few days before, when boning up to prepare for my meeting with X. Its main thesis, of course, swept far beyond Nolan's unhappy school days. It argued that large swathes of the Western visual arts could be explained as solitary but unrequited attempts of the artist at sexual satisfaction. Great art, according to Nolan, required the misfiring of a strong libido. It was perhaps hackneyed, but Nolan had saved it from banality in a variety of ways. First, he had not confined himself to analyzing "textbook" examples—if children are still taught such things in America's puritanical schools. He had raced past Schiele's forbidding lesbians, Dali's unnatural sodomies, and O'Keefe's flowery genitalia. Alongside these standards, he had marshaled less probable cases in point, such as Leonor Fini's women, androgynous and yet disappointingly heterosexual to a lesbian's eye. He had also devoted several pages to analyzing the Byzantine caricatures of a remarkably unholy patriarch. The man was shown exposing his deformed genitals in church, to a presumably baffled congregation, in order to acquit himself of charges of sexual misconduct.

Second, Nolan's piece had suggested a relationship between what he viewed as a marked decline in the quality of western art and the onset of the Viagra era. He had come up with an epigrammatic name for this theory: "can procreate, can't create." Meant tongue in cheek, it had nevertheless been swiftly ridiculed by a dissonant chorus of artists, art dealers and pharmaceutical companies.

Whatever his success at interpreting art history, Nolan's piece had managed to influence its course in a rather original way. In support of his thesis, he had surveyed the use of artists' excretions in modern art. He had started by pointing out that a number of artists, such as Andy Warhol and Andres Serrano, had experimented with urine. According to Nolan, the idea had actually been lifted from a Pasolini film of the sixties. Therefore, he had sneered, it could be described as fresh only if the particular specimen of Andy or Andres distinguished itself for an especially high ammonia content.

In a more daring burst of creativity, Nolan had continued, others had parlayed their feces into art. Manzoni, for example, had wisely done away with any manipulation and simply placed the material in jars for sale. Here again, Nolan had digressed to cite the lawsuit of an impatient heiress who had sought to have her art-collecting mother declared legally incompetent. The mother had spent vast amounts buying the product to which Napoleon's general Cambron had made his famous allusion. She was bent on amassing all authentic Manzoni jars. The expenditure had inhibited the daughter's purchases of less lawful but more pleasurable substances. The daughter preferred the "good shit," had punned a gossip columnist whose paper allowed itself greater license with four-letter words than the New York Times.

But, Nolan had concluded triumphantly, semen was the one excretion that had escaped use as an artistic medium, proving his theory that art was fundamentally inconsistent with gratification.

Sure enough, within a few days of the piece's publication the comment had sparked a "semen on canvas" exhibition. The raw material had been supplied by the angry young artists to whose presumed Viagra habit Nolan had attributed what he gamely called the "crappiness" of their work.

Joining the circus, the Women's Art Guerilla movement had decried the technique as an exclusionary use of the phallus by those creators who had one. The feminist organization then produced a poster that made its brief appearance in some of the more bohemian Manhattan neighborhoods. The poster's appearance was brief because it depicted the profile of a masked woman's head, her expectant mouth open below a paintbrush. The caption did not help defuse the sexual insinuation. "Semen for semen's sake?" it asked. This was a reference to the agenda of male domination that, according to the art guerillas, was hidden behind the motto "art for art's sake."

These were evidently women who had significant amounts of leisure time on their hands. I was sure, nevertheless, that both the semen paintings and the poster decrying them were duly counted in some line item of our economy's gross national product. Our society does not view such activities as any less meritorious than the production of milk.

The mayor tried to quash the poster, resorting to the usual incantation that innocent children would be indelibly marked by the sight. The guerillas countered in court that obscenity is judged by the standards prevailing in the local community. Ergo, nothing imaginable can be obscene on the streets of Noho. The ensuing Senate hearing made the name of an ambitious Republican, from a state with a name only vaguely known to the drama's East Coast protagonists. Nolan had many dinners on the story.

For the moment, of course, Nolan was looking forward to an imbibing of a more pleasant—to him, at least—sort than that evoked by the poster. He had already gotten hold of the wine list, always a dangerous book in the hands of this guest. At least I managed to confine him to the whites by invoking the fish.

For a while we attended to the culinary tasks at hand. We savored the amorphous mushrooms, rising from their humble subterranean beginnings to the top of Brillat-Savarin's hierarchy. Specialized dogs detect their unearthly smell, like talent scouts canvassing the slums for a poor kid who will go on to entrance the world as soccer star, tenor, rapper. And we ate the grilled *daurade*. Except for its price, Mediterranean fish is the most proletarian of delicacies. It does not need to be tampered with by sauces or elaborate preparation. It is equally delicious at the fish tavern by the beach or a three-star restaurant. Perhaps it also appeals to the eater's most barbarous instincts. The atavistic sight of the head on the plate seems to add perversely to the pleasure. The clear eyes signal unmistakably the recent-ness of violent death.

We engaged in some idle conversation about the war. Nolan was adamantly pro, the odd phenomenon of a Trotskyite apologist for the administration's actions. When I finally decided to broach the reason for our lunch, I did so gin-gerly. To make use of Nolan's reserves of knowledge, one had to refrain from venturing an opinion of any kind. He would be liable to interpret such overtures as an invitation to endless debate.

It proved not to be that easy. When I did ask Nolan what he could tell me about the picture, his immediate response was: "What can you tell me about it?" In fairness to him, I did need to provide him with some information. "Would it surprise you if I told you it was painted by Picasso in July 1937?"

"It would surprise me slightly," he said, in the languid accent that served both as his intimidation device and ticket to many Bordeaux-irrigated dinners around town. "But it would surprise me for different reasons than you may imagine. As you must know, the classicist manner has been a well-entrenched part of the Pic-asso canon since the 1910s. His work for Les Ballets Russes and the Rosenberg show in 1919 shook profoundly the cubist orthodoxy. The high priest and co-founder of the new wave had gone reactionary. He had reverted to the hated traditions of drawing and recognizable figures. Vociferous complaints of betrayal were made.

"Picasso was undaunted. He returned to the style off and on for the rest of his life. But there are indeed a couple of things that surprise me about your picture. First, the eye/tear is an unusual style break, even for a notorious mixer of styles.

"In case you doubted by the way," he continued, taking the copy I had e-mailed him and unfolding it on the table, "the eye is certainly a *Guernica* refer-ence. You said this was done in July 1937. I am reasonably certain that *Guernica* was unveiled in June or early July 1937, at the World Fair in Paris. He must have been working on both paintings at the same time. Look how the eye in your por-trait gravitates toward the earth. It's just like the eyes of most of the protagonists in *Guernica*—the bereft mother holding her dead baby, the man, even the broken statue. Do you know that the next-to-last state of *Guernica* had featured an actual tear? It streamed down from the eye of the hurrying woman on the right panel. Picasso removed it only in the finished painting."

"Why did he remove it?" I asked, although I was getting worried that we were straying far from Andrée.

"Most of the erudite scholars who have analyzed *Guernica* have missed the rea-son. They are blind to it for the usual reason—because it is so simple. When eyes have become tears, you don't want tears flowing from eyes. Picasso did away with the surplusage. The curious thing is that the hurrying woman is the only figure in the painting whose eyes have in fact *not* become tears. It is probably because she no longer carries a dead body in the finished painting, as she did in the early drawings. I bet her beloved is still dead. Picasso just doesn't want her to know it yet.

"But I can see I am boring you with things that need not burden your fine legal mind. Back to your original question, there is a second thing that strikes me about your picture. Picasso's classicism was mainly pastiche, exaggerated imitation of a slew of others. Ingres, Delacroix, even Rembrandt. They were all frequent targets. And the references were always very deliberate. This is what was missed by the appalled critics of the Rosenberg show. I saw Van Gogh, I saw Cezanne, one of them complained. I saw everything but Picasso.

"The reference here, however, seems to be outside his usual repertory of impersonations. If I had a guess, I would say someone like Jacques-Emile Blanche, an artist with whose work you would be excused for not being familiar. Blanche was a turn-of-the-century post-impressionist, better known then than now. He did the portraits of many illustrious contemporaries. The oval, pale face; the large eye. Yes, it certainly evokes Blanche. He is an underrated artist, in my view. As usual, the reasons have less to do with quality than with the advice self-anointed experts give to clueless shipowners. I would be glad to discuss his work further with you over dinner if you'd like," he concluded predictably.

I accepted his invitation to extend him another invitation, thanked him for his insights, and paid the bill. I walked back to the office. Crowds of other lawyers were likewise returning, from their three-iced tea lunches. I wondered what marketing genius had persuaded professional Americans overnight that iced tea was the lunch drink *de rigueur*, the new martini. Some lunchers coalesced in groups of older and younger suited people. This suggested an interview lunch, an event whose usefulness in Washington is compromised by the propensity of the interviewer to monopolize the conversation. They all looked languid. The combination of the sun and the digestive process seemed to have suspended for a few minutes the usual anxieties—I wonder who called while I was out, I wonder how I did. And none of them appeared to be entertaining thoughts of Baghdad or terrorism. On that sunny afternoon, Washington certainly did not look like the capital of a nation at war.

Lost in my thoughts, I almost stumbled into Superman, in full garb minus cape. It was in fact a messenger dressed in the formidable trade uniform of the tight-fitting Lycra suit. The look had recently been appropriated by white-collar joggers as well, like blue jeans climbing up the social ladder from coal miners to heiresses. But this guy was the real thing. He was standing by his bicycle on the sidewalk, a bag around his waist and a strange green scarf around his neck. And he was staring at me.

I apologized and walked on. I pondered whether the messenger profession had been dealt a blow by the Internet's more ethereal medium. I did not see as many of them riding around these days, their acrobatics a danger to cars and pedestrians alike. Which made me think again of X's prompt response to my e-mail about Nolan, and brought back my own anxieties about our progress on the project.

The lunch with Nolan had turned up another dead end. Andrée's portrait had been rendered in the manner of an obscure portraitist, if under-appreciated in Nolan's view. So what? Perhaps I should have Paul research Blanche and any relationship he may have had with Andrée. But the link was too tenuous to hold any promise. Despite my optimistic e-mail about Nolan's erudition, we still had nothing to show Mr. X for our efforts.

CHAPTER 6

▼

Little Marcel favored e-mail too. Late on the same afternoon, I received my first one from him. It came from the same hotmail address he had used to write to X. It was an even more laconic message, three words in fact: "*Aimez-vous Cabourg?*" "Do you like Cabourg?" Signed, again, "Your little Marcel." My new correspondent had immediately extended to the lawyer the same playful intimacy he had assumed with the client.

I knew Cabourg to be a seaside resort on the Normandy coast, close to Deauville. I had never been, because of a totally prejudiced aversion to all summer resorts situated on northern coasts. The memory of fierce winters appears to weigh on such places throughout the year. This creates a feeling that the brief periods of temperate weather are undeserved, almost stolen time. I found such guilt incompatible with the carefree spirit that must be part of a summer resort's essential atmosphere.

But little Marcel was not recommending to me a vacation destination. Nor could he be genuinely interested in whether I liked the place. He was providing me with a geographic clue. What had happened in Cabourg? Had Andrée lived there? Had she spent her summers there, riding and playing tennis? Was that where she and Pablo met? Was it the site of their affair, a romance so intense that Pablo had to immortalize his young companion decades after?

I dialed Paul's extension. "We have our first e-mail lead," I said. "Check all the book indices for Cabourg. Did Picasso spend any time there during the relevant period?" Paul, frustrated with the results of his previous searches, was not audibly excited by the new information.

"I will look," he said, "but what would this tell us? Assume we find that Pablo spent a summer in Cabourg. Then we must hypothesize that Andrée was there at the same time. Remember, we will not know that for a fact as her name does not come up in any of the reference sources. And even if we assume her presence, we will still know nothing. Only that Pablo and Andrée breathed the same sea breezes at the same time."

While I couldn't resist the customary force of Paul's logic, one assumption was better than two. And suddenly I had one more thought: "You might as well check whether Jacques-Emile Blanche spent time in Cabourg," I said. "He was a contemporary portraitist. An expert I asked believes Andrée's portrait was done in his manner. Please turn to it right away," I concluded, rushing to avert another justifiable discourse by Paul on the futility of that exercise too.

Paul appeared at my office door promptly after thirty minutes. "OK," he said. "Picasso did visit Cabourg a number of times. He was there in the summer of 1916 and again for a few days in 1918. I could not find much information about what he was doing there. And I could find nothing on Blanche and Cabourg."

So we had arrived somewhere, but were now at the precise impasse that Paul had anticipated—there was nowhere to go from there. I did ask Paul to check the Web, or perhaps call a French sports authority, for a list of equestrian and tennis events in Cabourg between 1910 and 1920. But I assigned that inquiry a very low probability of success. Had we been looking for baseball games taking place in any U.S. city over the same period, I was certain the information would have been readily available. But I doubted that the pride of the French in their history extended to the scrupulous recording of sports events from a hundred years ago.

I called my assistant and started dictating a memo to X. It would set forth the possible Cabourg connection. It would acknowledge (as I had to) that even that achievement had come courtesy of little Marcel. And it would essentially concede defeat. Then a frivolous impulse overtook me. Sure, X had discouraged me from attempting contact with little Marcel, but would he mind a little levity? I opened again the e-mail, pressed Reply and typed, in English: "Unfortunately not. Could you recommend any other destinations?" I hit Send.

That night I dreamt of a beach. It was not Cabourg. It didn't have the northern shore's guilt or pretense of insouciance. Rather, it was a Mediterranean beach. I knew because of the chant of the cicadas I could hear over the roar of the waves. I was lying on sand that was finer than pebbles but thicker than hourglass sand. I was in the animal state that can only be conjured up by the beach sounds and sensations. The cicadas, the waves, the sun feeling gradually stronger on the drying skin, combined to eradicate consciousness. Or, to be more precise, it was the ersatz consciousness of the dreamer that was being numbed into a daze. I wondered afterwards if, in all the tradition of western thought, there has been any philosophical movement focused on a day at the beach. Philosophers might be able to glean something essential about the human condition from that state of blissful anesthesia. I sun therefore I am. *Solito ergo sum*. But no such profound inquiry, let alone explanation, presented itself in my dream. I was simply dreaming I was half-asleep.

And then an unusual sound startled me from my sleep within my sleep. It was the trotting sound of hooves on sand. I opened my eyes and saw a young woman, about seventeen, riding a huge black horse. They were passing ten yards in front of me, moving from my left to my right. The horse stepped on the narrow zone where the surf came and went, making the sand more compact and therefore more malleable.

Again, philosophy may not have paid heed to this point of friction between earth and water. Nothing can be defined except with reference to something else, some philosophers tell us, and so on and so forth, until a vicious circle of relativity has been joined. Yet no one needs cross-references to comprehend the concept of this wet sand. It has the consistency children need to make castles, and nowadays, I suppose, more modern residences. It has the weight it takes to attach itself to the bare soles of our feet as a thin film. But reference to these qualities is necessary only to describe it in a book, not for anyone to understand it. How about a new philosophy, then, that is firmly built on this wet sand, like a child's castle?

It would have to wait for this philosopher's waking state. For the moment, my dream was continuing. On this sand, the horseshoes left imprints as perfect as they were ephemeral, a work of art destroyed by the next wave barely a second after it was created.

The horse looked like my mind's perception of Bucephalus, Alexander's beautiful black steed. The girl looked nothing like Andrée—her complexion was fair and her short hair was strikingly white. I caught a glimpse of beautiful large eyes and a French *retroussé* nose. But I couldn't discern in her face any of a teenage girl's piquancy or pertness. Rather, her features were organized into an expressionless mask of remote austerity. It was the sign of a woman who had learned early on that admiration was her due in life, so long as she did nothing to elicit it. She was topless, her small breasts barely bouncing with the horse's stride. But she displayed no self-consciousness, pride of doing something risqué, or vulgar expectation of attracting attention. She evoked the blasé attitude of a naked woman on a fashionable beach where nudity is an effortless choice rather than a rule of etiquette.

As she passed by, she seemed to spot someone to my right, and the mask abruptly dissolved. Her eyes shone, her face was brightened by a radiant smile, and she waved her hand. I turned in the direction of her wave, and saw a woman half-sitting, half-lying on a lounge chair about thirty yards away. Her features were obscured by large sunglasses and a monumental straw hat that reminded me of the catholic fashion show from Fellini's *Roma*. She was wearing a black one-piece swimsuit. She looked older, perhaps late forties, her body still taut. It must be the topless girl's mother, I thought in my dream. Notwithstanding the distance that separated us and my myopia when awake, I could discern the slender fingers of her left hand. The reason was perhaps that they were willfully yet lightly holding a long cigar. The elegance of the touch worked to defeat distance.

The mother seemed to acknowledge the girl with a slight tilt of the head, as if distracted. The girl proceeded to give Bucephalus whatever command is required to pick up the pace, and the horse started galloping toward the mother. But halfway, the girl abruptly pulled the reins and froze the horse to a halt, as if she had seen something that terrified her. I looked again in the mother's direction but saw nothing other than the woman with the hat and the cigar, now staring at the horizon.

Then the girl made a ninety-degree turn to her left, steering the horse right into the sea. The change of direction was strangely spasmodic. There was no psychological moment between stopping the horse and heading toward the ocean. She took no time to weigh the cause and effect of her impending action, or simply to ponder some desperate thought. My dream had robbed the spectacle of the more deliberative process one expects from life, or perhaps from the depiction of life in a Hollywood film.

And the journey into the ocean was also faster than normal in my dream's world. The horse could move in the water with the same speed as on *terra firma*. Soon horse and rider alike started being covered by the waves, then emerging again but for shorter and shorter intervals, until I could not see them at all.

I tried to get up, but could not. I turned to look at the mother. What I saw petrified me more than the sight of the disappearing girl, whose beauty was now cause for lament rather than admiration. The mother appeared entirely unconcerned about her daughter's plight, if she had registered it at all. Her cigar was suspending even more nonchalantly from her fingers. She was motionless like me, but not from fright. Rather, she seemed absorbed by the same languid preoccupation that had made her so lukewarm in recognizing the girl's enthusiastic greeting a few moments before. Her gaze remained fixed on the same distant point in the horizon, seemingly miles beyond her drowning daughter.

And then I came to the usual nightmare ending of waking up from a futile effort to scream. At least it was not a nightmare related to work, I thought. I turned on *CNN*, in the hope that the headline news monotony would serve as a lullaby. Not to be: the news at three o'clock that morning was laced with too much adrenalin to comfort an insomniac. Saddam had been captured. The world was awakening that morning safe from harm. The increase in our security was primarily theoretical, of course. It was not immediately clear whom the tyrant would have been able to harm had he remained in the decrepit hut where he was found. But it was no matter. All of our politicians, no matter how divided, united now in their applause for the utmost indignity. The proud dictator was forced to open his mouth for a doctor's inspection. The true purpose of the exercise was not hygienic. The billions of television viewers around the world needed to witness the thoroughness of his defeat.

I turned off the television and resorted to other sorceries to win again the favors of Morpheus.

CHAPTER 7

▼

"Aimez-vous Proust?" Do you like Proust? Little Marcel's second e-mail appeared on my screen early on Tuesday morning. This time he had not bothered to sign. Nor did he acknowledge my previous day's wisecrack of a reply, if he had even received it or understood it. He was readily identifiable, nevertheless, by his return address as well as his solicitous interest in my tastes, whether in literature or seaside resorts.

But perhaps he was after all responding to what he may have viewed—correctly—as a plea for help. Indeed, I immediately regarded this as a more promising clue than the prior day's geographical hint. It opened a broad vista of new possibilities.

Marcel Proust was more familiar territory than Cabourg. During more leisurely years, I had managed the feat of reading much of his masterwork, *A la Recherche du Temps Perdu—In Search of Lost Time*. After many more years of filling every square centimeter of my brain with court decisions, my memory of his long sentences had grown rusty, to be sure. It took two hours of Googling and reading the equivalent of cliff notes to reconstruct the gist of *La Recherche*.

The title was apt: in seven books, it tells the story of a narrator trying to find meaning in the passing time of his life. He searches in the love for his mother and grandmother. He looks in the smart society of duchesses and the aristocratic Faubourg St. Germain. He tries his luck with music and painting. He lays his hopes on his doomed love affair with Albertine. But all his searches are futile. He finds instead that life is robbed of meaning by the same thing that renders it livable— the numbing power of habit.

The only way to undo habit and touch reality is not a "way" at all. It cannot be willed. It cannot become a code of moral dos and don'ts or a "how to" recipe for living. And it can seldom be repeated. It is achieved almost reflexively by the senses, unmediated by intellect or conscience. It is the elusive moments of "involuntary memory." The taste of a madeleine soaked in tea brings back a summer tens of summers ago, and does so more vividly than we could live it at the time. The shock of a strange hotel room extricates us from the familiarity of our own bed. The sound of a fork falling evokes a long lost dinner companion more effectively than if she were to reappear and remind us of the mendacious promises we had made each other, or the food and wine we had. Except for those few moments, all time is inexorably lost.

I believe we all have had such experiences. A banal dance tune can awaken the sensations of our youth in a way that elevates us to a more intense state of elation than the highest of high art. I remember being transported in a Proustian manner to my childhood summers in Greece one day a few years ago. I was entering the apartment building where I was living then in downtown D.C. The transport means was provided by the smell of the new doormat lying in front of the door. The aroma of fresh plastic propagated itself to my nostrils in the uncommonly dry air. It was the resurrected smell of the swimming fins that my mother would bring out every morning at our summer house before we headed for the beach. At one point or another in our lives, we can all take credit, without trying, for feeling like little Marcels.

Little Marcels: so that was the message our correspondent had been trying to convey by his choice of pen name (or, as the French say, war name, *nom de guerre*). He had obviously guessed at our inability to get the hint. Or he had read my reply e-mail, and decided to become more explicit.

But for little Marcel this did not mean explicit enough. My initial euphoria about the possibilities opened up by the new lead gave way to anxiety over how numerous they were. *Vita brevis, ars longa.* In the case of Proust, not only was his work unusually long; his life too had become the subject of a cottage industry of biography. The results were even more voluminous perhaps than those achieved by the Picasso scholarship. Where to begin?

We had to discipline ourselves. I identified two promising areas of inquiry. First, the easier one: Picasso and Proust. Had the two masters met? When and where? Did they know each other's work? Second, the more difficult but also more intriguing one: *La Recherche* had always been viewed as a *roman-à-clef*, a novel with a key. Most of its characters corresponded to actual figures of Parisian society. I suppose every novelist must look to those around him for inspiration.

But Proust appeared to have done so with such abandon that it put him in hot water with many of his friends. For my purposes, this had a fascinating implication. Could Andrée have been one of the book's characters, perhaps its protagonists? And could that role in turn hold the key to a real event that took place more than fifty years after Proust's death—the defacing of her portrait?

In my overexcited mind, the first and most fascinating possibility was Albertine, the woman whom the narrator loved. Her story is among the central building blocks of *La Recherche*. Insanely jealous of her suspected lesbian dalliances, the narrator keeps her practically imprisoned in his house. She finally quits him only to further devastate him by her untimely death. But then I remembered: Proust was one of the twentieth-century's most famous homosexuals. He patronized male brothels. He enjoyed the torture of rats for its apparent overtones of anal penetration. He jumped from one boyfriend, real or aspired, to another. It was well established that the basis for Albertine's character was a man, a pilot by the name of Agostinelli who died tragically when his plane crashed.

So we had to look elsewhere. Gilberte, the young daughter of Swann and Odette with whom the young narrator had yearned to play? Odette, her high-class courtesan mother? The duchess of Guermantes, the beautiful socialite in whose house he had longed to be admitted? *La Recherche* was in a sense the story of the narrator trying to gain access to a number of unapproachable men and women. He would eventually succeed, only to be disappointed when they failed to live up to his expectations. At this point, Andrée was also unapproachable for me. I wondered whether discovering her secrets would prove a disappointment similar to those that had inflicted the narrator.

But in any event, the field of candidates was vast, and no time was to be wasted. So I summoned Paul to my office and gave him his new assignments. Number one: Proust and Picasso. Number two: the narrator and Andrée.

Other projects occupied me until about three in the afternoon. Exhausted, I decided to take a break for a couple of hours, a decision that was greeted by my secretary with a customary quizzical look. I left the office and walked the two blocks to my house.

It was a clear autumn afternoon. I took in the low-rise Victorian townhouses, the office buildings jutting out between them, the deciduous trees, the pedestrians, the joggers and the clueless squirrels. In many Washington neighborhoods, these heterogeneous sights form a delicate ecological balance between the willful and the natural. There is a harmony between the angst of professional accomplishment and the colors of the falling leaves that other world capitals might do well to emulate. On this afternoon, however, the balance was violently upset by the intrusive sound of a police helicopter hovering above the rooftops. It was an increasingly recurring nuisance in these times of homeland security. The same sound, from Blackhawk military helicopters, was probably disturbing the sleep of the residents of Baghdad at the same moment. But what was here a vague menace was there a foreboding of much more likely disaster, for innocent civilians and innocent helicopter crews alike.

And then a squirrel throwing a nutshell in my path helped cast these depressing thoughts aside. For the first time, I was feeling mildly optimistic about our strange little project bearing fruit, so I decided to enjoy my break.

CHAPTER 8

▼

When I returned at five o'clock, I found Paul already in my office waiting, pacing up and down. This time he was ebullient.

"Well," he burst as soon as he saw me, "we have an answer. To both questions. And more." In his excitement the promise of the "more" came out sounding like the high C note in an aria. At last.

"First of all, Marcel and Pablo did meet. There is at least one instance recorded by Painter, Marcel's seminal biographer. It was at a party given by the Schiffs, a wealthy English couple, patrons of the arts, in 1921. It seems to have been an extraordinary gathering, as it was attended by a number of twentieth-century superstars. Aside from Marcel and Pablo, James Joyce and Diaghilev showed up. Presumably Nijinsky was there, too, but Painter does not say. Also, Marcel knew and liked Pablo's work. He was bemused by the infatuation with cubism that had seized the fashionable women of his circle. In fact, Pablo makes a cameo appearance in *La Recherche*. 'These ladies,' the narrator says, 'touched by art as if by heavenly grace, lived in apartments filled with cubist paintings, while a cubist painter worked only for them and they lived only for him.' And in a preface he wrote for someone else's art book, he speaks of 'the great and admirable Picasso.' He has particular praise for Pablo's portrait of Jean Cocteau. 'When I contemplate it,' he says, 'even the most enchanting Carpaccios in Venice tend to take a second place in my memory.'"

I remembered the occasion of the Schiff party from my Googling of Proust. I had found accounts of it focused on the convergence of Proust and Joyce, the two greatest writers of the century. The point of these descriptions was an astonishment at how these two geniuses, each responsible for rivers of great words, hardly exchanged a word except for banalities about the weather. I thought the premise was naïve. The idea that the two had missed an opportunity to cross-pollinate at some exalted level betrayed a lack of familiarity with the solitary rites of creation, not to mention the institution of the dinner party. Proust did not even have good conversational English, and I did not know the quality of Joyce's French. Perhaps we should have expected the fireworks to be set off by a meeting of the two men's translators. Come to think of it, this was another story told from the viewpoint of the sports fan, like the coverage of the war in Iraq. The world's two best teams meet, and spectators expect the greatest game ever. But they are disappointed when injuries on both sides prevent the players from reaching their potential, and the match ends in a scoreless tie.

I was more interested in who else was at the party. "Any chance that Andrée may have been a guest?" I asked Paul.

"Wait," he said. "There is another link. Cabourg. Marcel spent many summers there. In fact, Cabourg was the basis for Balbec, *La Recherche's* fictional seaside resort. And Marcel was there in August 1916, at the same time as Pablo."

"So, is this where they first met? And was Andrée there?"

"I think so," he said triumphantly. "At least as to the second question. In fact, I think I know who Andrée was." Paul was enjoying the prospect of exceeding my expectations.

"You asked me to find a character from *La Recherche* that appears based on Andrée," he continued. "I think I have found the key. The key is that there is no key. Andrée was Andrée. Albertine's best friend. One of the band of laughing, athletic girls that the narrator encounters in Balbec. She was the woman whom the narrator suspects of being romantically involved with Albertine."

So, I thought, that was it. The hardest things to find are the ones that are not hidden at all. Andrée was Andrée. Not a protagonist after all. More of a bit player. But that explained the tennis and the horse riding. It explained why that early twentieth-century Amazon was comfortable in a man's domain, why she excelled at contests where women take on men. It explained, too, why she remained single. Andrée was a lesbian. Perhaps she was also the woman-man profile depicted next to her more conventional likeness in Pablo's picture. Could the picture be a double, or triple, portrait of the same person? Was that its hidden meaning?

But then I remembered that, in Proust's distorted world, the lesbian relationships were hidden code for heterosexual ones. The real target of Marcel's jealousy was Agostinelli, whom he had transgendered into Albertine, and *his* relationships with women. That would make Andrée straight after all, one of Agostinelli's girlfriends. Perhaps she never married because she never recovered from the shock of his death in the plane crash. Andrée's smile in the picture from *Le Figaro* became even more poignant in my mind, as it was proven oblivious to a tragedy more imminent than her own death—that of Agostinelli. The rest of the 1910s were going to be a trying time for the victorious smiling woman.

"And by the way," Paul concluded, in a certainly pre-planned *coup de grace*, "I mentioned the art book to which Marcel contributed a preface discussing Picasso. The book was entitled *From David to Degas*. Its author was himself a painter: Jacques-Emile Blanche. Marcel and Blanche knew each other well. In fact, Marcel's best known portrait was painted by Blanche. Here, have a look." He opened the Painter book at a page marked by a Post-it note. I looked at the portrait. It featured the signature moustache, the black hair, and, most prominently of all, the mesmerizing dark eyes. It was the same gaze as that radiating from Andrée's single classicist eye in the portrait—and, come to think of it, from Picasso's own eyes in the photograph. Nolan was certainly right. The manner of Picasso's rendering of Andrée was the same as that in Blanche's portrait of Marcel. Same oval, pale face highlighting the eyes. Only the vertical eye/tear, the style break in the Picasso work, set them apart stylistically.

So it had finally come together: that was the encrypted message in Picasso's choice of style. Pablo was telling us about Andrée's place in Marcel's world. But why? And why did someone not want the world to know?

Here, thanks to Paul, was our first concrete advance in the project. To be sure, the unknowns still outnumbered the knowns. But the knowns were no longer zero. I started composing a status memo to X very different from the one I had feared I would have to write. I detailed Paul's discovery of Andrée in *La Recherche,* explained the Cabourg and Picasso-Blanche angles, and began to list the open questions.

CHAPTER 9

▼

The distorted Sphinx was staring at me from the two eyes of her frontal profile. The colors of her face had nothing to do with flesh. Dozens of her facsimiles surrounded me as if in a hall of mirrors. She was not Andrée; she was Fernande, Pablo's first muse. For some reason I had received an invitation for the *vernissage* of the Fernande Olivier portrait exhibition at the National Gallery taking place that Tuesday evening, and decided to go. Perhaps I entertained a stupid hope that a hidden message in the portraits would help connect some more dots, from Fernande to Andrée. Did Fernande know Andrée? I wondered. Had she too spent time in Cabourg, with Pablo? And did she know Marcel? I made a mental note to ask Paul the next morning.

Fernande did not say a word to me, of course. She remained Sphinx-like in the immobility of her uncomfortable poses. And nor did anyone else. I did not know anyone in this crowd. Washington is a mosaic of heterogeneous communities, each gravitating around one of its centers of activity. The lobbyists do not know the lawyers, who do not know the diplomats or World Bank people, who do not know the venture capitalists. I had no idea which of these groups the other guests belonged to. Most of them were dressed up. The ensemble looked rather like an opera crowd. It was a far cry from the usual armies of tourists frequenting the place, their aesthetics apparently unaffected by the art on display. Museum visitors are akin in that respect to our flip-flop wearing airport crowds, who do not appear to bring back from their travels anything like Odysseus' riches of experience.

Paul was there. I caught a glimpse of him, walking with his characteristic limp toward the exit. He must not have seen me. I was a little surprised to see him. I knew that Paul was an art lover, but I didn't know his short tenure in Washington had already bred the kind of connections that result in such invitations. Perhaps he had elicited one hoping to get the same thing I was looking for—an insight of some use in our project. I knew Paul remained the consummate professional in all his waking hours. I hoped his visit was more fruitful than mine.

And then I saw X. In fact, I almost bumped into him, like the bike messenger the day before. Maneuvering among the crowd to get from a pointless point A to an equally pointless point B, I came upon the commotion that can often be observed around men of power. Power has its physics too. It disturbs its immediate environment into peculiar formations by emitting a strong magnetic field. But for some reason X's entourage had left his front exposed, and so I found myself directly facing my client.

I knew that he was not going to use the occasion of a party to ask me about my progress on a project that he obviously viewed as highly confidential. For a moment, I rather wished that he would. I was eager to share with him our discovery of Andrée's identity. But I remembered that I had not yet completed the status memo, let alone placed the partial answer we had found in a coherent whole. On balance, therefore, I decided that jogging X's memory about the fact of my existence was not a good thing at that point. It might trigger a phone call from him first thing next morning. I nevertheless had no choice but to mutter a deferential hello, and prepared myself for a few minutes of awkward pleasantries.

But it was no matter. X was looking right through me, or rather at some point to the immediate left of my head. My concern with reminding him of me gave way to a new one: was my client deliberately disregarding me? Maybe he was afraid that acknowledging me would make some fellow guests ask themselves why he needed my services.

But when I turned to follow his eyes behind me, I realized the explanation was much simpler. X was ogling two women standing a few yards from us. One was wearing a black evening dress. Her bare back was turned to me. "Statuesque" was the literal word to describe that back. The shoulder blades, like low hills sloping down the ravine of her spine, had the color and consistency of Pentelic marble, Pheidias' raw material. They also had the inevitability of a work of art, and the sensuality of a new kind of non-obscene pornography. Stiletto heels catapulted her six-foot frame above the heads of most other guests. Her short hair, cut "*à la garçon,*" was curiously white. Her left hand was holding a tiny handbag, with which she seemed to be caressing her neck. It created the strange impression that she was whispering sensual nothings into her cell phone and at the same time speaking in a normal tone to her audience of three or four.

The woman's right arm languished possessively around the waist of a slightly shorter companion, whose beauty I could appreciate more clearly, as I had a clear line of sight to her left profile. Dark-haired, she had the fathomless enigma of the Eurasian face, the drama of the high cheekbones. She was a modernized, and perhaps slightly Asianized, version of Andrée. In fact, I thought I recognized her from somewhere, perhaps from television or the movies. Her own black dress, equally generous with her flesh as that of her friend, was slit at the side. It revealed a leg that looked as if it had been extended unnaturally on a Procrustean bed. If so, this Procrustes could justly be proud of his gruesome work.

So this was the ultimate billionaire's trophy. *Droit du seigneur* or, rather, *du milliardaire*. All the pleasure of possessing small pieces of canvas with triangles on them, all the thrill of being ushered to the best tables by subservient *maîtres d' hôtel*, paled compared to the possibility of such a conquest.

And, sure enough, the besieging was underway. One of the men in X's entourage broke out of his group, walked in the direction of the brunette and tapped her lightly on her bare right shoulder. She turned her head, so that her right profile was now visible to me. She looked surprised, as if she had been shaken from a trance. The man leaned and whispered a few conspiratorial words in her ear. But she did not appear interested in conspiring. No response registered on her facial muscles, not even an inquisitive arching of the non-existent eyebrows. The man redoubled the effort. His hands now gestured emphatically, making duty for what would be a more persistent tone if he were not still whispering.

So that was X's method of courtship. He did not use his henchmen only to fire, intimidate, and do the distasteful things that billionaires with charitable aspirations no longer want to dirty their hands with. He used them also to procure for him.

But this was not his night after all. His seignorial expectations notwithstanding, the vicarious advances did not seem to produce an effect this time. The woman finally turned further to the right in X's direction, her spine and long neck the only repositories of motion in her body. Standing a few steps to X's left, I could now see both her eyes and their impassive stare. They did not evince preoccupation, at least not of the kind that had caused X to disregard me only a few minutes before. Rather, they gave the odd impression of piercing him blankly, like two high tech missiles that have been stripped of their nuclear load and evoke violence only by their aerodynamic lines. After gracing him for one second with this sublime indifference, she turned back to her white-haired companion, who had never let go of her waist, and to the men in their group.

I thought it best not to distract X from his collecting interest of the moment, especially since it was so far from being gratified. Nor did I want to embarrass my client by making him aware that I had been a spectator to this short pantomime. I retreated back into the crowd, browsing the enigmatic painted woman instead of the living ones.

Another half an hour passed before I headed out. The breeze struck my face. It gave me presumably the same sensation felt by the president, senators and other prominent Washingtonians who may have happened to spend some time in the open that evening. Weather is another constant, like the sun and the sand. Or is it the only absolute that we can directly feel, the symbol of God on earth? When we say "it's hot," "it's cold," "it rains," "it snows," what do we mean by "it"? Does language fail us before these phenomena? Weather is the "it" that cannot be penetrated. Perhaps this makes it the measure of everything, like the gold meter kept under lock and key in Paris, the only object about which we cannot say whether or not it is one meter long.

A fleet of black town cars lined the cobbled driveway between the two buildings of the National Gallery, waiting for the slowly departing guests. Most of them were too well-heeled, and in the case of the women too high-heeled, to entertain the idea of a cab or Metro ride home. Suddenly, above the non-descript murmur of the idling engines, there rose an altogether different sound. It was the roar of a motor that was built to rotate much faster than that of the town cars. But it did not produce the brash obnoxiousness of a NASCAR muscle car. Rather, it evoked the louche decadence recognized by anyone who has spent time at certain strategically located cafés in Monte Carlo. It was the signature sound of the high-tuned Italian thoroughbred, telltale of fast money and fast play. I turned my head to the right, and saw it came from the four exhaust pipes of a sixties-shaped, blue two-seater. A trident adorning its tail, the car was positioned at the head of the line, priming to disappear into the night. I could make out the outline of a passenger, but could discern no more in the glare of the lights falling on the right-hand door. On the side farther from me, however, the driver's window was obviously open, for a man was leaning against the door. He was talking with the invisible driver, or rather listening to him, as the man's own mouth was not moving.

I squinted and was surprised to recognize Superman, the biker that I had collided with two days before. Or at least it was someone who dressed and accessorized in the same way. He held the steering wheel of his bicycle with his left hand. His Lycra outfit clung to his body, and the same bright green scarf circled his neck. He took a package from the driver. He then got on his bike and vanished beyond the illuminated driveway into the relative darkness of Independence Avenue. Seconds after, the car's engine finally ripened into an explosion, propelling it like a zigzagging missile in the same direction.

CHAPTER 10

▼

"*Aimez-vous* Nabokov?" Do you like Nabokov?

Great. Little Marcel's new missive arrived early Wednesday morning and was waiting for me when I got into the office. Just when his last e-mail had allowed us our first true break, here was another little clue of no obvious relevance whatsoever.

I started to question the integrity of little Marcel's motives, even his seriousness. Up to that point, I had pictured him as a basically benevolent *deus ex machina*. He was playful for sure, but he was nevertheless trying to help us in his tough-love way. He seemed like the nurturing teacher who holds part of the answer back so that the kids will use their brains to discover it themselves. But his latest salvo suggested instead the sadistic streak of a prankster taking pleasure in throwing us off.

Who was this guy? What was his relationship to the mystery? He certainly had some inside knowledge. Otherwise how could he have had access to the photograph of Picasso with the portrait? And how else could he have pieced together the connection between the defaced face and the woman featured in an obscure obituary notice from *Le Figaro*? Imparting that information to us had certainly earned him some legitimacy. But that did not preclude a change of mood, a decision to stop being helpful, or a little joke at our expense.

In any event, whether clue or prank, we had to leave no stone unturned. The problem was that this particular stone was sitting on more mountains of data that we would have to find our way through.

Vladimir Nabokov, another titan of twentieth-century literature. Little Marcel seemed to be taking us on a very educational tour. I had read some of his books, and more Googling quickly uncovered the basic facts of his life. He was born in Czarist Russia. His father was a distinguished civil servant. His family was uprooted by the Bolsheviks and moved to Berlin in 1917. He studied at Cambridge and returned to Berlin in 1923. Throughout his stay in England and Germany, he made frequent trips to Paris. He ultimately moved to Paris in 1937. He was one of many Russian émigrés who found themselves in the reverse American dream of riches to rags—from a privileged existence to a more humble *train de vie*. We would have to check carefully that period of his life. In 1940 he moved to the U.S. In the 1940s and 1950s, he taught literature to college girls. One or more of them must have provided the inspiration for the novel that won him worldwide fame—*Lolita*. Thankfully, I thought, there is not yet a Son-of-Sam type law that forbids professors to earn royalties from books inspired by lust for their students. Otherwise, some of the most resonant pages written in English in the past century would never have been produced.

So, another foray into the life and work of another sacred monster. I called the hapless Paul. By now, I was sure, my capable associate had started longing for the dry legal work from which he had initially been happy to escape. "Same drill," I said. "Let's find the Paris facts. Was there any interaction between Picasso and Nabokov? They may have moved in overlapping bohemian circles in Paris. Same for Nabokov and Proust. I doubt that Vladimir would have had access to the rarefied salons that Marcel had finally broken into by that time. But Marcel too had a number of circles. And wasn't Vladimir a handsome literary young man at the time? Marcel might have solicited his company for a combination of intellectual and sensual reasons. And finally, of course, was there any Andrée Duplessis in Vladimir's life?"

With Paul gone off to our new quixotic quest, I turned to another important task. I had to record the time that I had devoted to Mr. X's project so far. As even the most legal-trouble-free person will know, lawyers charge by the hour. This means that they have to describe the work they perform in time increments. The difficulty is that most of what we do revolves around thinking. We think about what to write or say; we try to understand what we read. This makes the recording of time a fundamentally arbitrary exercise. What was I thinking at 11:05 this morning? And how do I cast that thought in concrete terms (write, read, look for things) to make it more palatable to the client? It is a dismal method. What if Proust and Nabokov had similarly had to describe the time spent in producing their work? Thinking about young boys. Thinking about young girls. Those would have been the most likely descriptions.

Oddly, lawyers are often maligned for charging too much per hour or charging for too many hours. But they have brought these criticisms upon themselves. They feared that the previous method of charging for their services (based on value added for the client) would be seen as too subjective. So they came up with an "objective" method, trying to account for the unaccountable.

Mr. X's project posed a particular challenge in this area. How to describe the time spent pursuing the chimeras that little Marcel kept placing in front of us? I decided the solution was simple. I would go by Marcel's successive directions: "Attention to Cabourg. Attention to Marcel. Attention to Vladimir." Who knew what the next entry would be. I hoped that Mr. X would not run our invoice by his army of accountants.

CHAPTER 11

▼

The hotel bar's walls were paneled from floor to ceiling in richly colored wood, done in "faux-something" style. The décor displayed the innocence of an imitation whose author does not quite know what he is imitating. Something old, something old-world, something British. Perhaps a library in a country house, *sans* books. But no particular period has been picked as a frame of reference. No design books have been consulted to ensure the accuracy of the general idea. Thus the project actually acquires a degree of modest originality and a romantic approximateness, like the castles of Disneyland. The result in this case was neither tasteful nor completely tasteless, with the unhappy exception of the horse prints.

Horse prints seem unavoidable whenever new America looks for inspiration to the land from which its first citizens shed so much blood, sweat and tears to extricate themselves. Art has made great strides in the last century and a half to escape from the photographic depiction of reality—strides of which this hotel decorator seemed unaware. The painting of horses, however, has actually moved in the opposite direction—that of more realism. This is because photography has shown us a surprising fact: the galloping horse's two pairs of legs converge when in the air. Contrary to the prior belief, they do not distend away from one another. That revelation would have dumbfounded the painters of the abhorrent pictures on the walls of many American hotel bars. It couldn't have surprised an experienced horsewoman like Andrée, I thought, even though her riding years must have been at the cusp of this paradigm shift.

Nolan was already there, seated at a corner table, striking the usual discord with his surroundings. This evening, his stocky frame was clad in a brown corduroy jacket. His corduroy trousers were a shade of brown that was not similar enough to qualify the ensemble as a suit, and yet was not different enough to avoid a sartorial disaster. His customary silk scarf, this time blue, was tucked into his shirt. The David Niven touch both heightened the inelegance of the whole and strangely moderated it. The look became almost a daring fashion statement. He had started working on a bottle of malt whiskey, cradling an unusually small glass in his hands and sipping contentedly.

"Sit down, my dear fellow," he said, "have a drink. I specially asked for the small glasses. Do you know that large whiskey glasses would drive the Duke of Windsor into an incandescent rage? The wretched man was a cretin in all large things, but he had a kind of idiot savant genius for all things of no consequence." Nolan's far left ideological leanings had not interfered with the British fixation on the eccentricities afforded by privilege. If the Bolshevik revolution had successfully expanded to England in the early twentieth century, the English brand of the socialist state would probably still have featured a hereditary king. He would still be going around shaking his comrades'/subjects' hands, dressed in red plaid kilts.

Nolan had called my office earlier in the day suggesting drinks. This surprised me slightly, as we had already scheduled dinner for the following week, but I accepted. I did not have any plans, and I still nourished a slim hope that he might be of help in my project. Half a bottle of whiskey later, however, nothing of any relevance to it had come out of his mouth. Instead, the alcohol, of which he had a definite lion's share, had helped us settle into the easy mode of conversation that often makes acquaintances better company than friends.

The lack of anything essential in such relationships appears to have its own light but irreducible essence. Importantly, they are guilt-free. We would not be expected to sacrifice ourselves for our acquaintances. So, when dealing with them, we do not have to contend with doubts over whether we would truly sacrifice ourselves for our friends.

Not that casual relationships are appealing only because they are frivolous. Frivolity is unquestionably one of their most pleasing characteristics. But they can also afford moments of depth and sincerity that we often do not hazard with our close friends. To be sure, the tone is different from that struck in conversations with friends and, for that matter, in our professional dealings. The sincerity is not dressed in its usual cloaks of bathos ("you know I would never lie to you"). It is not compromised by the desire to appear considerate. Nor is it used as a weapon to humiliate or defeat a professional adversary. There is no need for the dreaded "let me be frank," which serves both as a preface to a hostile remark and as a device to redeem the hostility by investing it with a virtue. Candor can have its own peculiar hypocrisy. But it is less adulterated in social relationships where we have little at stake.

My conversation with Nolan this evening was not an exception from these rules, or so I thought. It was wide-ranging and typically lopsided. Nolan could safely be expected to use more, and longer, words than any interlocutor. As usual, he copiously vented scorn at various manifestations of American culture. This was a staple of any conversation with Nolan on American soil. When in Europe, he switched to praise for what he sometimes termed a "refreshingly American" view.

He also brought up religion. An atheist, Nolan had a strange fixation on the canonization process of the Catholic Church. He had, in fact, embarked on a campaign to reinstate the position of the devil's advocate or, in Vatican parlance, "Defender of the Faith," abolished by the church in the 1980s. According to Nolan, this "tragic event" had led to scandalous travesties of justice. With no prosecutor to cast them in the worst possible light, several candidates had attained sainthood without being saintly at all, and in some cases without even having performed the required number of miracles. "Remember," Nolan said, "the devil's advocate does not in fact advocate the interests of the devil. He defends the faith. God is his client. If no due process is given to God," he concluded triumphantly, "why should any be given to the poor Al Qaeda suspect? From the kangaroo proceedings of the Vatican to the detentions without hearing at Guantanamo, it is a short path indeed."

I ventured to object to what seemed to me a meteoric leap. But Nolan plainly did not see it as a leap at all. "What do you think, my dear fellow?" he scoffed. "All political wars are first fought in the arena of religion. And they are decided there, before the guerilla gets up to fight, and certainly before the voter wakes up to vote. Art, of course, is another matter. It was much less effective than religion at capturing the hearts and minds at the best of times. But things have gotten worse—nowadays art cannot even *interest* any heart or any mind. It is inevitable really. Gallery shows can never approach the solemnity of mass. I read the other day that Playboy magazine is putting on the block Dali's auto-sodomized virgin. I ask you, my dear Melanchthon, if a variously penetrated virgin has no resonance for Playboy magazine, does art have any power at all? It is a sad state of affairs."

Nolan's foray into surrealism, as well as his surreal transitions from one subject to the next, must have encouraged a crazy impulse in me. "Let me ask you something," I said. "Imagine a young woman on a horse, riding into the sea, to her drowning. Her mother is watching. Does it ring a bell?"

"Sounds surrealist enough for anyone to have done it. Dali, Magritte, Delvaux. Is this another one of your artistic projects?"

"No, it is not a painting," I confessed with some embarrassment. "Just a dream that I had a couple of nights ago."

I did not know what I was doing, and why. I seldom have dreams that I even remember, except in the vaguest possible way. I have always been baffled by the accounts of famous artists writing down convoluted dreams every morning to draw inspiration from them. Perhaps artists are induced to vivid dreams by necessity—precisely the need to conjure up material for their "job" of artistic creation. I, by contrast, have found dreams to be of little use in the practice of law. Whatever the reason, having few memorable dreams has made me reticent to acknowledge my amorphous dream life to myself, let alone discuss it with others. But my recent dream certainly stood out—it was both detailed and memorable. And lawyers do have the tendency to impart confidences to unlikely recipients. This is usually because a meeting happens to be on their calendar after they are struck by a private insight or crisis. The rhythms of professional life sometimes make unexpected confidants of all of us.

My embarrassed admission certainly gave Nolan a chuckle. "My dear man," he said, "my expertise does not extend to dream interpretation. I can offer you neither a psychiatric nor a magical insight. I do suspect instinctively that I would favor the coffee-dregs reader over the shrink. Perhaps you could consult your ancient compatriot Artemidorus. It would probably be more productive than therapy. It does appear to be a banal dream, if I may say so without offending your subconscious. Whiffs of Lady Godiva. But I have always thought that a true dilettante should not disclaim any kind of expertise. At least not unless life or limb are at risk from pretending to be a doctor or a firefighter. So, since you ask, three things do come to mind.

"First," he started after taking a sip, "I recall another compatriot of yours, of more modern vintage, committing suicide in this rather extravagant fashion. Pericles Yannopoulos was his name. He was a poet, but don't feel bad if the name doesn't say anything to you. Decidedly minor in his poetry, he aspired to grandness in his death. So he rode a white horse into the ocean—or the sea, as you Greeks prefer to call it.

"Number two, you seem to share a dream life with Katherine Harris." I blanked. Was this a new artist, whose name was common currency in the *avant garde* circles frequented by Nolan, but had not yet reached that most rear of guards—Washington lawyers?

"You do not recognize the name now, but you would have in 2000. This is the problem of ephemeral fame. Katherine Harris was the Secretary of something for the state of Florida. She was in the middle of the controversy over vote-counting in the 2000 election. Her nights were apparently no less frenetic than her days during that period. She had dreams. In one of them, she confided to friends, she saw herself riding a horse into a stadium full of republican fans and delivering the trophy of victory to them. I am not certain how her dream squares with her duties of impartiality. I suspect the American legal profession has developed a legally protected freedom to dream, established through a lot of expensive litigation. In any event, I read about it in a book. Apparently one of her confidants did not have a friend's discretion, or else it was meant for publication from the start. You, of course, have no reason to worry. Your dreams are safe with me," he said sardonically, reminding me of my own foolishness. "By the way, the horse color was not specified in the account, but I wouldn't be surprised if it had been white in the original dream."

In fact, I had no faith in Nolan's secret-keeping abilities. The exposure of private facts to the public eye is after all the essence of any journalist's job. But the risk from Nolan's natural urge to tell a funny story at my expense was minimized by my lack of celebrity, ephemeral or otherwise. It is interesting, I thought, how politicians seldom speak about their dreams, except metaphorically. "I have a dream" perhaps, but never "I had a dream last night." Only daydreams, it seems, are politically safe. Political discourse has changed since the more mystical times of Joan of Arc. Yet politicians surely have them, and some must remember them. When a president one day chooses to break the rules and speak of *his* riding a horse, it will surely make the front page of the papers, and give a tricky hermeneutical job to the writers of the editorial page.

"Number three," Nolan continued undaunted, "your dream reminds me of something I saw on TV a few evenings ago. I was watching an overlong documentary on Leni Riefenstahl. The general idea was how terrible it was for her to have placed her art at the service of the Reich, as if it would have mattered one way or the other. She denied doing anything like that, of course. She also said that she had spurned the advances of Joseph Goebbels. I found that hard to believe. The chief of Nazi propaganda and the chief Nazi propagandist. Sounds like a match made in hell. A match more poignant than you may imagine."

Goebbels. How was he relevant to anything? Nolan was truly the master of digression.

"No, don't worry," Nolan continued, guessing my impatience. "I suspect few National Socialists documented their dreams, and certainly she did not in the documentary in question. My emphasis was on overlong. I soon grew weary of watching an octogenarian watch large fish underwater, although I have to say that Leni's taking up scuba-diving at that age does present a certain psychological interest. It suggests the need to cleanse oneself. Puts the lie to the claim that she was unrepentant.

"In any event, I resorted to the idle switching of channels, a practice I believe is called flipping in households that practice little else. So I came upon another documentary. This one was on Federico Fellini. The director affectionately called *il mago* by the Italians was being interviewed about the secrets of his magic. It turns out Fellini had a recurrent dream. He often dreamt of the other master illusionist—Picasso. In the dream as he described it, Picasso offers Fellini an omelet at a seaside hut. He then proceeds to swim into the ocean, inviting Fellini to follow suit. Soon, only Pablo's bald head and big hands are visible. Note, incidentally, that if Picasso had been born without legs, he wouldn't have been disabled at all. He would have been the opposite of disabled. All his potential would still be there unscathed, in the head and the hands. And yet who knows what would have become of him. Perhaps he would have become even greater. One would have to assume that his sexual drive would have been more fettered."

I could see a seed planting itself in Nolan's head of a way to buttress his "procreate, not create" theory in the face of its main bug. The flaw was, of course, Picasso's sexual appetite. It was gargantuan, yes, but according to all accounts it was also gratified with great frequency. I remembered that Nolan had tried to explain away the problem in his piece by resorting to dark intimations of impotence— bizarre considering the master's multiple offspring.

"That was it," Nolan concluded. "Fellini then explains that this does not mean a specifically 'Picassian' influence in his moviemaking. Rather, he says, he dreams of Picasso as a generic symbol of creativity. I was surprised by the adjective, by the way. I thought the correct form was 'Picassoesque.' Having your name become an adjective is certainly a mark of admission into a pantheon of sorts. I suppose an adjective with two different suffices signifies an even more exclusive inner sanctum—a VVIP room."

I saw Nolan's eyes wander nostalgically, surely to a point in the horizon where "Nolanian" converged with "Nolanesque" to affirm for posterity the greatness of Christopher Nolan, author, connoisseur and conversationalist. "Picassoesque" was certainly the adjective preferred by Chairman Lower in his dissent. But he had hardly used it in a way to suggest that the chairman was admitting Pablo in his or any other pantheon.

I did remember seeing the Fellini documentary myself. So perhaps my dream was connected to work after all—to the subject matter of my assignment from X. It had merely undergone one of those transformations whose illogic has created so many professions to interpret them—professions in the fields of magic, science, and religion.

"A propos of which," Nolan continued seamlessly, "were you able to get any additional intelligence on your Picasso?" My professional guard returned, the malt whiskey notwithstanding. My plan had been for any such intelligence to flow in the opposite direction—from Nolan to me.

"Hardly," I said, a near-no that was unfortunately truthful. "Have you had any ideas?"

"Well, not ideas in the platonic sense," Nolan replied. "But I did come across something that might interest you. A 1937 Picasso oil was auctioned this past spring at Sotheby's. A hermaphrodite portrait, half man half woman. It had nothing in common stylistically with your work. It was done in what you might call generic cubism. Except for the palette. The colors of the two works seemed very similar to my untrained eye. Same blue, same grisaille, same striking orange. I could be mistaken, of course."

Nolan's false modesty was getting on my nerves. If he had truly believed his eye was untrained, he would never have admitted it. I could nevertheless not help admiring his perspicacity. He was on to X's secret. Neither the vandal's hand nor my secretary's artful Xeroxing had helped conceal from him the association between Andrée's face and the rest of the work. In some awe, I dumbly stared at the man with the super-trained eye, who was now taking another sip of his drink. Alcohol consumption had on Nolan's speech the imperceptible effect that it often has on seasoned British drinkers. The slur only makes their accent sound posher still. It is as if the open-voweled accent was invented to mask precisely this kind of infirmity. Perhaps Englishmen of a certain class train their facial muscles to mimic willfully the state of relaxation engendered involuntarily by a fifth glass.

"In fact," he continued offhandedly, "the work ended up in our neck of the woods, according to art world gossip. It seems that the buyer is one of our local, if not indigenous, tycoons. None other than X. Do you know him?"

The casual sound of the remark made me all the more nervous. Despite his vast preference for talking over listening, I was sure that Nolan was an old hand at offhandedness. As a journalist, he must have had some training in the interviewer's art—eliciting damaging admissions under the pretense of innocuous conversation.

"I know of him," I said humbly, neither denying nor affirming any personal acquaintance. "I understand he is a person of enormous wealth."

"Yes, it is certainly enormous, if it is his," Nolan mumbled.

"If it is his." The theatrical device of the dramatic aside involves a murmur uttered on stage. It is supposedly inaudible by the other characters and yet it is heard by an audience of hundreds. The laws of acoustics are not conducive to the verisimilitude of this device. Rather, it is based on the convention that the other character on the stage has either become momentarily deaf or has always been a total idiot. Nolan's coda paid obvious homage to this implausible convention. In this case, I seemed to be both the intended audience for the aside, and the idiot supposed to believe that it was a private remark not intended for my ears.

"What do you mean?" I took the bait. I recalled the vague Internet rumors of X's shady dealings. Was Nolan implying that X served as a front for someone shadier still?

"Nothing, my dear fellow, just the old Marxist in me. Ownership is theft and all that. I work, you work, X pockets. In any event, I'm sure he is a hard man to see, but you might want to try. He may be able to shed some light on the color association between the two paintings. Perhaps you could lure him by suggesting that a little mysterious backstory might add millions to the market value of his work. Few things tempt a man more than the prospect of becoming richer without any effort. It's like flouting some primordial law of nature against windfalls, eating the proverbial free lunch."

Nolan should know. Free lunches and dinners were a temptation to which he never refrained from yielding. I didn't want to continue this dangerous conversation. I changed the subject, awkwardly but not without a certain cunning. A question about the particulars of Nolan's theory of artistic creation was bound to refocus him on his favorite subject, that of his underrated genius.

Another ten minutes of bombast elapsed. I was not truly critical of Nolan's self-absorption. It was nothing more than an exaggerated caricature of the most fundamental human trait. Imagine that the Department of Homeland Security decided to wiretap the tables at all of Washington's restaurants and bars, in its zeal to keep citizens secure from diners and drinkers. What secrets would the resulting thousands of hours' worth of tapes reveal? Few that would be useful, or at any rate that could be deciphered in time to avert another catastrophe. But the taxpayers' dollars would not have been wasted. The expensive endeavor would make our ace wiretap analysts wiser to an essential truth: that self-love is the fuel of all conversation. The businessman brags about his brass-knuckle tactics. The lawyer tries to convince of his powers of persuasion. The well-bred man tries to score points by his modesty. The non-profit player relies on his altruism. The powerful man can afford to be magnanimous, confident that his sycophants will do his bidding. The men are worse than the women, and only the terrorists remain silent.

Not that self-love is exclusively a Washington phenomenon. It afflicts the French, too, or at least it used to in the seventeenth century. When I was eight or nine, my French teacher, Madame Nicole, had me memorize a maxim of *La Rochefoucauld* that I parroted for years but didn't really understand until adulthood. "The modesty of men in the most elevated positions is an ambition to appear greater than the things that elevate them." Nolan's immodesty was at least more sincere, and he practiced it with brio.

I finally asked for the check and made my excuses, leaving a content Nolan to savor the remaining jiggers of the malt. It was about eleven o'clock and raining lightly when I got out of the hotel. Oddly, the temperature had risen. In fact it felt hotter outside than it had inside the bar, despite the thermal energy released by a burning fireplace, burning cigars and warm bodies. It was as if an ecological cataclysm had befallen the earth during my conversation with Nolan, endowing Washington with a tropical combination of heat and rain in mid-November. But this particular climatic disturbance proved more directly man-made than the obscure links of cause and effect in the religious debate over global warming. It was caused by the powerful radiator hanging from the awning above me and extending the hotel's shelter to patrons waiting for their cars.

In truth, the idea was not comfort, but rather the luxury of waste. Outside heating is a little like the trappings of leisure—a tan and sunglasses. They became fashionable not because they were intrinsically appealing or fulfilled a need, but because they signified someone who could afford to be idle. This is also why tanning salons would seem to be such a characteristically American phenomenon. They feature three of the most salient traits of American materialism: the love for efficiency; the indifference between the authentic and the fake, so long as the result looks the same; and the disregard for huge expenditures of energy.

Washington, of course, was suspicious of tans. It viewed tanning salons, to which a busy politician might repair for a semblance of vitality, as only slightly less disreputable than brothels. The nation's capital put a premium on pallor.

Lost in my thoughts, I started walking the few blocks to my house. The raindrops now fell more steadily on the large golf umbrella that the doorman had helpfully lent me. I crossed the street and, right in front of me, saw a woman I recognized. It was the Eurasian brunette on whom X had lavished such unreciprocated attention at the National Gallery. She was naked, but alas, not in the flesh. Rather, she was enlarged about three times and in facsimile. Her picture adorned a giant billboard, strategically located to block the view of the shabby gas station across the street from the hotel—one of the eyesores that predated the area's gentrification. So this was why she had looked familiar to me.

The picture shone in the evening in luxurious black and white. The Tahitian cheekbones cast dramatic shades on the lower part of her face. Her body was thin but sculpted—small breasts, the interminable legs I had already noticed, the slightest *hanche*. It was halfway between the non-existent physique of couture models and the more muscular ideal cultivated by health clubs.

Despite the brilliant nudity, however, her eyes were the picture's clear focus. Her defiant stare into the lens had neither kindness nor malice. It radiated the moral certainty that one rarely sees in photos of people from more respected professions, such as politicians, priests or captains of industry. It was the cool calm of someone with nothing to hide. I suspected that, in fact, models were in no less need of flattering camera angles and digital touch-ups than politicians are in need of mendacious spin. I also knew that good-looking women are more insecure about their appearance, on which so much of their self-perception hangs, than plain-looking ones. But neither doubt nor inhibition clouded this naked woman's eyes.

The only color on the poster—red—was reserved for the investment bank that the model had improbably been hired to promote. The names of the bank's two founders and the prosaic ampersand between them covered incongruously her erogenous zones. Subliminal brand-building. The lack of any rational nexus between product and message had become one of the advertising industry's less endearing habits. Judging from myself, I was sure it was ineffective, too. I knew of no recesses in my mind that would slowly convert the woman's flawless nudity into some concept of banking transparency. But perhaps that was the point— that I didn't know.

I walked on, but something kept nagging at me, as if the poster had a significance that I had missed. It was not until I reached my doorstep that I realized what it was. Black and white. The copy of Andrée's portrait that I had shown Nolan was black and white. I didn't even have a color copy.

CHAPTER 12

▼

In the office Thursday, other pressing matters arose throughout the day—matters that, for reasons of attorney-client confidentiality, do not warrant mention in this chronicle. At about seven in the evening, after several calls and meetings, I remembered I had not yet heard back from Paul. I suppressed with some difficulty the usual partner impulse of bombarding the associate with calls. It is a tactic as fruitless as it is frustrating to the calls' recipient. Career advancement means doing to people at the step below the things you hated done to you when you were there. It is the opposite of the Christian golden rule.

I turned to the *CNN* Web page. Christian values were being vigorously invoked, by no less than the president. He was holding a press conference, facing increasing pressure from the media over persisting post-war casualties in Iraq. He said that he prayed for the dead and their families. He reassured Americans that this was a necessary sacrifice for the greater good, the goal of Iraq's liberation. He brushed aside aggressive questions about the missing weapons of mass destruction. He temporized when asked why we had not found any. He didn't explain why the administration's reasoning for the war had shifted from weapons to liberation. He said he was going to address the United Nations in New York on the coming Tuesday.

I did not blame the president. He had a difficult job. He was saying the same things that all presidents had said before him and, doubtless, all would have to say after him. Ever since Thucydides, the big open question of every war has been who started it. Who was at fault when the first sword was brandished, the first shot fired, the first nuclear bomb detonated? The question is never really going to be answered. Who can calculate how many people have died at war since the start of history? Millions? Billions? Romans used to pour salt on the battlefields to purify them, or cover the stench of death. I wondered whether there was an equivalent modern practice.

It was already eight in the evening. I had turned off the lights in my office and was getting ready to head home when Paul appeared, holding books. He reached to the light switch and turned it back on. I had seen a smile like his before. I realized I was thinking of Mr. X's triumphant grin when he was alluding to his conspiracy fantasies.

"I think I have the answer," he said. "We had it all wrong."

I offered him a chair, but he was in a state incapable of sedentary immobility. He started pacing around the office. The excitement had even made his limping somewhat more pronounced.

"I hit all the biographies of Vladimir's early years," he said. "From what I can tell, Vladimir did not know Pablo. He did not know Andrée. And he did not know Marcel. But"—right index finger in the air—"he wrote about Marcel. The answer is not in Vladimir's life; it is in his work. Read this."

He handed me one of the books he had come with. It was a paperback edition of *Ada or Ardor*. He explained it was one of Nabokov's last novels, and pointed me to a paragraph he had bookmarked on page 168.

"Before you start, let me give you some context," he said. "The super-educated young Van is in incestuous love with his super-educated young sister Ada. Van visits Ada at her boarding school. He takes her to a 'milk bar,' whatever that is. But they have to be escorted by Ada's undereducated chaperone, Cordula. Then Van starts talking about Proust."

I started reading the paragraph. Van was talking:

> I would like your opinion, Ada, and yours, Cordula, on the following literary problem. Our professor of French literature maintains that there is a grave philosophical, and hence artistic, flaw in the entire treatment of the Marcel and Albertine affair. It makes sense if the reader *knows* that the narrator is a pansy, and that the good fat cheeks of Albertine are the good fat buttocks of Albert. It makes none if the reader cannot suppose, and should not be required, to know *anything* about this or any other author's sexual habits in order to enjoy to the last drop a work of art. My teacher contends that if the reader knows nothing about Proust's perversion, the detailed description of a heterosexual male jealously watchful of a homosexual female is preposterous because a normal man would be only amused, tickled pink in fact, by his girl's frolics with a female partner. The professor concludes that a novel which can be appreciated only by *quelque petite blanchisseuse* who has examined the author's dirty linen is, artistically, a failure.

I read a few lines down. The undereducated Cordula's response was: "Ada, what on earth is he talking about? Some Italian film he has seen?" Ada's reaction was to mutter, "You've had too much Marcel." My own reaction combined that of the sister and the chaperone. What on earth was Paul talking about? He had evidently had too much Marcel—and too much Vladimir. I just stayed silent, looking perplexed at my colleague.

"But don't you see?" Paul asked, impatiently. His voice now started shrill and proceeded to become shriller still as his sentences unfolded. He reminded me of some rabble-rousing orator in prewar Europe.

"This is our key. Van is wrong. He says that Marcel's jealousy over a lesbian affair would be preposterous if he were straight, because heterosexual men are titillated by lesbianism. But I went back to read Marcel. I took the story at face value. I pictured Albertine as Albertine instead of Alfred Agostinelli. And the point is, it is *not* preposterous. Because, first of all, jealousy *is* a natural feeling for a man suspecting his girlfriend of being a lesbian. But second and most important, it is not only jealousy that Marcel describes. It is jealousy mixed with titillation.

"Marcel hated Albertine's love affairs. But he also hated himself for being irresistibly attracted to them. Why else would he have gone on about them at such length? To be sure, jealous men, straight or gay, torment themselves with fantasies. Where is their boyfriend? Who is their girlfriend with? But usually the fantasy stops at the bedroom door. Anything happening beyond becomes unbearable to contemplate. When you read Marcel, however, you can't help the impression that he would have liked to enter the bedroom and watch. And do you know that the first scene of gay sex that Marcel describes in *La Recherche* is between women, not men? The young boy narrator watches from a window in amazement as the daughter of Vinteuil, the composer, and her girlfriend engage in some sadomasochistic play-acting. Does *that* appear preposterous to you? Doesn't it sound like the fascination of a very heterosexual young boy? And why would Marcel devote half of Sodom and Gomorrah, the homosexuality book of *La Recherche,* to lesbianism, if he was not titillated by lesbians? Sodom for gay men, Gomorrah for gay women. I do not know of many gay men who take such an ardent interest in lesbian sex. I do know of many straight men who do. Marcel was heterosexual, or at least bisexual."

"What's your point, Paul?" I asked, still trying to catch up with my junior associate and not being altogether happy about it.

"Andrée Duplessis is not Andrée. She is not Albertine's friend. She is Albertine."

The phone started ringing. Paul paused, either for breath or for dramatic effect. I remained speechless.

"Do you know how Albertine dies in *La Recherche*?" Paul picked up his thread. "She falls from a horse. Everybody thinks that this was a stand-in for Agostinelli's plane crash, but the truth is simpler. Albertine falls from a horse because the woman who inspired her had fallen from a horse. Andrée did not die, of course, but Marcel knew he had lost her for good. I think her absence from his life was so painful that he had to equate it with death—the ultimate confirmation of lost time. And, by the way, read the account of Albertine's death. It is among the least persuasive parts of *La Recherche*. Only the riding accident rings true."

"Paul, this is brilliant," I finally said, somewhat jealous myself. "But it still appears speculative, don't you think? You have done a great job, but the evidence is still scant. If this were a legal theory you had come up with, I would ask you for more case law."

"And I would say I have found it," he said, undaunted. "First of all, I am not alone. Painter had already suspected the truth, without being altogether conscious of it. Here's what he says on, let's see, page 115 of the second volume." Paul took off his glasses rather dramatically and started reading to me:

"'It was during this visit'—he means to Cabourg—'that Proust met the mysterious young girl whom he also saw from time to time in Paris and, a year later, thought of marrying. Not even her name is known, although she may be alive to this day'—he writes that in the 1950s. "I suppress her identity," wrote Antoine Bibesco—one of Marcel's friends—"as she has begged me not to print her name."

"And at page 153," Paul continued, "he quotes from a letter written by Marcel in 1916. Timidly, as if he does not want to jinx his good luck by presenting it as a certainty, Marcel writes about the possibility of his engagement to the mystery girl. "'A person who is dear to me,'" he calls her, and adds: "'perhaps you will soon be hearing news of me. Or rather, I shall ask your advice. To make a very young and charming girl share my horrible life, even if she is not afraid of doing so—would it not be a crime?""'"

Paul closed the book. "Painter was right. The young girl, whose anonymity was guarded by Marcel's friends to the end, was still alive forty years after. She would live for several decades still. In fairness to him, Painter did acknowledge that she may have been a partial inspiration for Albertine, together with Agostinelli and others. But he was too caught up with the preconception of Albertine as Agostinelli, exactly as we were, to connect all the dots.

"And let's look at that preconception," Paul continued. "You ask me for evidence supporting my theory. What about the evidence supporting the Agostinelli theory? There is none, it is all speculation. Here is Painter again, let's see: '*Perhaps* Proust hurried Agostinelli to Paris in August 1913 because he detected him in a seaside flirtation.' When the narrator listens to Albertine singing in the bathroom, according to Painter, '*no doubt* it was Agostinelli whom Proust heard here humming.' Albertine is riding a bicycle? 'Proust is thinking of Agostinelli bowed upon his steering wheel.' Why would anyone see a man driving a car in the description of a girl riding a bicycle, unless he was straining to prove a prefabricated idea? And listen to this: Albertine says to the narrator he has opened for her a new world of ideas. Here are Painter's acrobatics: 'The same apparent change had occurred in Agostinelli, and the same pathetic words were no doubt spoken by him.' It all sounds like Bob Woodward divining the thoughts of presidents and cabinet secretaries in his peculiar genre of non-fiction. But would it have one chance in court?

"And there is more," Paul continued. "I have the hardest evidence of all. I have Marcel's smile." He opened the first volume of Painter to a photograph and showed it to me. Marcel was posing in tennis whites, holding a racket as if he was playing the banjo. He was surrounded by three girls. "Look at the young girl to the right," Paul said. "She must be about ten or eleven. Painter places the picture in 1891 but he is wrong, it must have been taken in the 1900s. Because the girl is Andrée. Here, look at the young equestrian from *Le Figaro*."

I could not deny the likeness. Same oval face, same cheekbones, same eyes.

"Is there any other picture of Marcel smiling?" Paul asked. He put his glasses back on, as victorious as Andrée holding the prize. "And is it a coincidence that Andrée Duplessis also figures in it?"

Paul was right about one thing. The mock-banjo-playing Marcel in the picture looked a different man. He was in a vastly better mood than the melancholy Proust pictured in Blanche's portrait, which Picasso had dexterously adapted to give the same melancholy expression to Andrée.

"So there is no question in my mind," Paul concluded. "Andrée Duplessis was Marcel's best hope for capturing time. Losing her devastated him and confirmed *La Recherche's* hypothesis—all time is lost. Our Andrée was responsible for the completion, if not the first spark, of one of the greatest masterpieces ever written."

We heard a deafening peal of thunder. It sounded like a message from Zeus, a divine affirmation of Andrée's identity and contribution to humanity. But I realized after a moment it was in fact the vacuum cleaner, deployed by the armies of cleaners that seize downtown offices every evening.

Notwithstanding the vacuum cleaner's imprimatur, I was still not one hundred percent convinced. Paul had combined ingenious speculation with some circumstantial proof, but I still felt more was necessary. There were, after all, two other girls in the picture. Paul had completely glossed over them. And there were other gaps. We would certainly need to do some research into any psychoanalytic studies of men's reactions to lesbianism. But most of this was clean-up work. It could be left for later. In truth, I was greatly impressed by Paul's theory. I agreed it was supported by at least a preponderance of the evidence. It was time to move to the next step.

"So," I said, after congratulating my young colleague. "Where does this take us? How does Andrée-Albertine fit into the puzzle of Pablo's portrait and its defacing?"

"Well, to begin with, it is clear that Pablo, Marcel and Andrée met in Cabourg in August 1916. I think the 1937 portrait must evoke in some way that meeting. But I admit that the message Pablo was sending is still very much an open question."

And suddenly it struck me: the cookie in Pablo's hand in the photo was a madeleine; the hourglass in Andrée's hand in the portrait was the symbol of passing time; and I remembered the Greek etymology for *clepsydre*, the French word for hourglass and title of the portrait: stolen water. Stolen time. And the *Guernica* eye/tear? Andrée was shedding it over the loss. What about the androgynous profile? Perhaps Marcel and Andrée facing different ways, the union that was destined to be ruptured.

Pablo had gone far beyond copying the manner of Marcel's portraitist: he had encoded *La Recherche* in a few masterly brushes shortly after completing *Guernica*. And he had then had his photograph taken with a madeleine in hand, standing in front of the painting, lest there be any doubt about its meaning. But someone wanted that message to be forever lost, and we still did not have a clue as to why.

CHAPTER 13

▼

Friday morning started with a sense of optimism. For lawyers, this is often caused by the absence of voice mail blinking on the phone set as they enter their office. Notably, there were still no calls from X. I logged on and started browsing the Web before getting to the business of the day. The first order of business would be to revise and expand the status memo to X. I needed to detail for the client Paul's discoveries from last evening.

The news was not good. Murder was rampant everywhere. Suicide bombers had struck in Istanbul. Many more dead in Iraq from all sides—American, pro-American Iraqi, anti-American Iraqi. How difficult it must be for our soldiers to tell the ones from the others—those who meant well from those who did not mean well at all. When the Catholic forces took back the town of Beziers from the heretical Cathars in the thirteenth century, the Catholic leader went straight to the local abbot. He asked the holy man how they could tell Catholic from Cathar. "Kill them all, my child," the abbot answered. "God will recognize his own." All in all, the collaborating Iraqis were at the greatest risk. Their allies mistrusted them and their compatriots detested them as a fifth column.

The president had to make an additional brief appearance to steel the nation's nerves. More comments about necessary sacrifices. At the UN on Tuesday, he would make the case for the war of yesterday, the occupation of today, the liberation of tomorrow. He would ask for help from our alienated allies.

Mildly depressed by the news, I decided to indulge in a further short break. I went down to the local coffee shop for my first espresso (*ristretto*) of the day. It was one of those habits to which, according to Marcel, we become unconsciously enslaved. But there was no escape. *CNN* was on, albeit on mute, at the shop. The all-news network was delivering a double whammy. The closed captioning titles were superimposed at the top of the screen, the headline tape wormed its way through the bottom. The top was all Baghdad, the bottom all Istanbul. The combined impact was somehow more eerie than if the sound were on and the announcer could be heard talking, rather than seen mouthing gruesome lines in a silent horror movie.

I gulped down my liquid breakfast and started walking the fifty yards back to my office building. And then I heard a voice behind me, gradually magnified as if someone was turning the volume up on a loudspeaker.

"Sir. Sir. Mr. Melanchthon." I turned and saw Superman, rapidly approaching. It was certainly the bike messenger that I had almost stumbled on after lunch with Nolan the other day, and who had picked up a package from the mysterious sports car driver at the National Gallery. This time he almost bumped into me. He stopped his bicycle from what seemed to be an extraordinary speed just a few inches behind me on the sidewalk. Why was Superman lunging at me like a rocket? Was it a puerile act of revenge for my earlier absent-mindedness? But how did he know my name?

I looked at him. His dreadlocks were the product of intricate weaving. He had spent much less time grooming the bushy black beard that covered most of his face. He still wore the green scarf that I had noticed at our first encounter. And then I recoiled. On closer inspection, I realized that the scarf was an enormous python, wrapping itself in several rings around his neck. Pet, heating device and possible death angel, all in one. Or perhaps it was a plea for God's protection. "Aegis" is Greek for goatskin. It was the snake-ringed scarf that Zeus had lent to Athena for her protection. What subterranean stream had linked this twenty-first-century bike messenger directly to the superstitions of Athenians from two and a half millennia ago? Presumably, he put the snake in his bag, together with the assorted pleadings he was carrying, before approaching the unsuspecting receptionists at his client law firms. I noticed, too, that the color of his eyes was a cold reptilian gray. Pet and master do become alike over time.

"Message for you, Mr. Melanchthon," the biker said. He handed me an envelope and sped away, the python tail hanging on his back like a punk, green ponytail. He left me no time to ask him anything about the sender's name and peculiar choice of transport means.

But no worries—the name was scribbled on the envelope: "To Mr. Melanchthon from little Marcel." My correspondent, wherever in the world he happened to be, had chosen to vary his delivery methods. And to judge from the English on the envelope, he was bilingual after all.

I opened it. It contained two glossy color photographs. I looked at the first. Its subject needed no introduction. It was Picasso's magnum opus. *Guernica*. It was hanging from a white museum wall. But there was something jarringly wrong about the iconic canvas. It was defiled by huge red graffiti. They extended across the entire length of its lower part. They covered the baby that lay lifeless in its wailing mother's arms; the arms and head of the fallen statue; the horse's legs. The spray-painted words read, in irregular capital letters: KILL LIES ALL. To the left and right of the painting, a number of uniformed NYPD officers were trying to ward off an obviously agitated crowd. The commotion suggested a real act of vandalism, rather than photomontage.

I turned to the second photograph. It was *Guernica* again. It was vandalized again, but this time by someone who had charitably done his handiwork on the photo instead of the picture itself. Now a speech cloud with a tail, like those used in comics, emanated from the pointed tongue of the horse that dominates the work's central panel. It spanned most of the painting in length, this time covering the mother's face and sparing the child's. It contained seven words, written calli-graphically in red:

"Equestrians know not to step behind horses."

The words were followed by a red cross. It was a cross that did not inspire prayer, because of the tiny lines protruding at a ninety-degree angle from each of its edges. A swastika.

I felt as if the espresso had exploded in my stomach, sending reconstituted cof-fee beans in all directions, like a napalm bomb. I rushed up to my office. I ignored the chitchat about the weather that secretaries feel compelled to exchange when riding the firm's elevators. I walked speechless past my own perplexed assis-tant and closed the door behind me.

Murder. This is what little Marcel was telling me, not so subtly. The nonage-narian's death was not an accident. Andrée was not only defaced in effigy but actually murdered. Someone had pushed the poor lady behind the horse. I imag-ined her wrinkled features contorted by dread. I saw the melancholy face of Pic-asso's portrait turning into the terrible face of Edvard Munch's screaming figure. I realized that I had not seen any picture of Andrée as an old woman, and won-dered whether her killer recognized the young girl in his victim's tired face.

Murder, or at least so little Marcel wanted me to think. My thoughts turned to my increasingly unpleasant correspondent. Why was he tantalizing me? If he was right, how did he know? And what secret was worth killing Andrée to pro-tect? Certainly not our theory that Andrée Duplessis and Marcel's Albertine may have been the same person. It was interesting, if true, and no doubt of earth-shattering importance to the quaint community of *proustomanes*. But *La Recherche* was, after all, a novel. People do not kill over the key to a "novel with a key." Perhaps our discovery had another dimension, at once more consequential and more sinister, that we were totally missing. Perhaps it placed our lives, too, at risk.

And what about the swastika? What did the Nazis have to do with Marcel, or Pablo? What did they have to do with Andrée? Was she killed by a demented neo-Nazi, in Paris in 1995, half a century after Nazi boots had made their last goose step marks on the boulevards of the City of Light?

The project was not going well at all. For lawyers, unlike soldiers or firefighters, violent death is not an occupational hazard. I should have told X no when I could. I should not have succumbed to the temptation of a new client that law firms, Mephistopheles-like, teach us never to resist.

I tried to restrain myself from a complete descent into absurdity. Logic must prevail. I took in my surroundings. I ran my hand across the glass surface of my desk. I surveyed my sparse office. It aspired to be like X's but it did not succeed. The clean lines of the furniture were at constant risk of erosion by an ever inflating, but somehow calming, ocean of paper. I concentrated on listening to the heating vents emit their sweet murmur, so reassuring that habit made it inaudible. I thought of the unsung achievements of climate control in suppressing the smells of paper, ink and graphite that law offices start betraying when the system goes off after hours. I sought shelter in the image of my protective assistant coolly screening and dispatching calls outside. I tried to prick up my ears to the quiet buzz of legal business being conducted on my floor.

All my senses bore testaments to rational efficiency, to the fact that Baghdad and mayhem were thousands of miles away. Or were they the cocoon that Marcel had discovered we cannot extricate ourselves from? And was that cocoon pierced by little Marcel's little message? Did he have it delivered by the python-embraced biker because he wanted to immunize it from the anesthetizing effect that electronic transmission has on our receipt of bad news? Were his dark intimations of little murder a reminder that larger murder was never that far away after all?

It was the work of the day that finally disciplined my paranoia. Letters, filings, phone calls, the comfort of familiarity that customary actions can conjure up even more effectively than customary things. The memo to X, and the disquieting thoughts it would doubtless trigger again, would have to wait till Monday.

Normalcy had more or less taken over again when I left the office for home around six. Men and women in crumpled suits were converging into the mouth of the metro station. They were heroically preparing to be swallowed by the modern-day subway Pluto, who would debouche them into the Elysian fields of their suburban homes.

Others were headed for nearby bars, to participate in the custom unhappily referred to as "happy hour" or, on Friday, "TGIF." The ritual unquestionably has many American peculiarities. Alcohol plays its American role of eagerly awaited release from a day's bottled-up pressure. The moralizing puritan indulges his vice of choice. But it also evokes an old French habit—the "*cinq-à-sept.*" The bourgeois functionary spends time with his mistress between 5 and 7 before returning home to his wife for dinner. Another overlooked similarity between the two nations' psyches.

Next to me, at the pedestrian crossing halfway between my house and office, a woman wearing a sports bra was running. Or rather, she was jogging in place, waiting for the light. I had always suspected this practice as an act of moral reprobation for the bystanding, non-jogging pedestrian, cloaked under the guise of some athletic expediency. But the woman seemed quite oblivious to me and devoted to her exercise, which had certainly achieved for her the desired results. Her bare stomach was totally flat, nothing but formidable muscle.

My thoughts were obliterated by a stentorian sound—the buzz of the patrolling helicopter. Have those machines ever succeeded in their advertised purposes? Have they ever helped stop a terrorist or catch a perpetrator? More likely, they are designed to combat crime by the psychological device of alerting us to its menace, making it audible. If so, the sound certainly had on me an effect close to its intent. It started sinking me again into the morning's gloom, an omen of bad things about to happen.

And then, not fifty yards from my house, I heard the shots. Ta-ta-ta. They hit the sidewalk right behind me. I ducked and fell on the ground. An acute pain was piercing my Achilles' tendon. As I fell, I caught a glimpse of a silhouette, running and disappearing into the narrow side street.

I looked up and came face-to-face with the shooter. The neighborhood's delinquent black squirrel was staring impassively from his perch down at me and at the lethal nutshells lying nearby. And I realized that the furtive shadow must have been the flat-stomached woman. She was jogging on, unaware that, for one moment, she had been viewed by a man from behind as a totally undesirable assassin.

I was going crazy. I collected myself. Stumbling, my strained calf muscle notwithstanding, I ran home as fast as I could.

CHAPTER 14

▼

I was sleepless throughout most of the weekend. When I did sleep, I had night-mares. The melancholy Marcel was holding a banjo in one hand. With the other, he was dragging a smiling, bare-breasted Andrée toward the horns of a giant bull-horse. Pablo stood by, madeleine and cigar in hand. He was laughing and shedding a tear. A miniature Blackhawk helicopter was hovering over a lesbian embrace. The disembodied woman's side of the cubist profile was kissing Andrée on the mouth. The tear had finally left Andrée's eye and was now running down her cheek. Perhaps this dismal state of affairs was what Chairman Lower had scornfully described as Picassoesque.

When not dreaming or despairing, I tried to reread some passages from *La Recherche,* particularly the Albertine books. I searched in vain for more clues. But the exercise did achieve a useful purpose. While it still did not convince me entirely, it did gradually erode my doubts about Paul's theory. It was not so much that I started picturing Albertine as Andrée. It was more the realization that I had always pictured Albertine as someone like Andrée, certainly as a woman, even when I "knew" her to be a man.

Prompted by the verisimilitude of the first photograph in little Marcel's mis-sive, I also did some Web research into *Guernica.* Sure enough, it was not a trick. It had happened when *Guernica* was still the pride of the Modern in New York, before it was turned over to Spain to mark the death of the *Caudillo* Franco and the return of the country to democracy. The painting had fallen victim to the precise act of vandalism recorded in the photo. The perpetrator was a man who aspired to create an art happening out of a shocking assault on the established art order. And doubtless, to create a name for himself.

Such people have always existed. Herostratus burned down the temple of Artemis in Ephesus, one of the ancient world's seven wonders. His goal was to gain posterity for his name. In that he succeeded. The Ephesians tried to frustrate his goal by meting out an eccentric punishment. No one was to ever utter his name, on pain of death. But, predictably, the injunction proved impossible to enforce.

The *Guernica* vandal, for his part, had no evident plans on posthumous fame. He favored the sweeter intoxicant of celebrity during one's own lifetime. In that, he too succeeded. He apparently monetized his notoriety into an established position in the New York art world and a gallery bearing his illustrious name.

Happily, his handiwork on the painting had less effect than Herostratus' on the temple. The fresh spray-paint proved easy to remove without any lasting damage. De Kooning had been less lucky in the hands of Rauschenberg, who had erased a drawing of the abstract expressionist and exhibited the result as his own work in the 1950s. Rather masochistically, De Kooning had given his consent to the erasing, in contrast with Picasso and the goddess Artemis, who had not been asked. I wondered how much this artifact would fetch at auction today, and whether it would be priced as the De Kooning that it had been or the Rauschenberg that it became.

Vandalism as art. Perhaps the two are less distinct than they appear. Perhaps Andrée's defiler was a would-be artist himself? In fact, who knows? The defacing of Andrée could have happened in the same period as the spray-painting of *Guernica*—during the decadent seventies. Was this another clue sent my way by little Marcel? Could the perpetrator be the same person, or at least a follower of the same demented art cult?

At about four on Sunday afternoon, I lit up my first cigar of the day. I don't remember whether I have mentioned my cigar-smoking. I smoke the long, slender panatelas. Pablo favored the thicker Churchills, such as the one in the picture. Indeed, he once sculpted one from wood.

And then, perhaps compliments of the nicotine euphorically entering my system, I had an idea. NART. North American Research and Technology, the mystery seller of the picture. A missing link, perhaps the missing link. NART must have known something about the picture's prior provenance. NART may also have known about the defacing. It had never been established when the painting was vandalized. It may have happened on NART's watch.

True, X had distinctly signaled that I should not worry myself with NART. The who will flow from the why, otherwise I would have hired a private investigator, he had said. But how could I find him an answer? How could I ultimately serve my client, if I stayed confined in the impenetrable Sanskrit of books about books? How could I content myself with the insinuations of sadistic little Marcel as my most authoritative source? What if it was the other way around? Maybe the why flowed from the who. And what if NART was the who?

I looked NART up on the Web. It provided incomprehensible technological solutions, to problems that its customers had probably not appreciated they were faced with. "Integrated." "Optical." "Total." "Solutions." In our service economy, this distance from anything concrete was more reassuring than suspect. All of my clients were in the service sector; many of them had clients who were service providers too, and so on. It took several degrees of separation to reach something that could be described as a "good." Most of our gross national product was not a product at all. It could no longer be caressed, broken or discarded.

The bursting of the dot-com bubble had finally infused a dose of reality into the ether that our economy had become. I had personally survived the market melt-down unscathed, thanks to the lawyer's conservative instincts. Speculation was never for me. I had not amassed, but I had accumulated. My capital had continued to breed capital. A windfall inheritance from an aunt had also helped. I would never attain Croesus's freedom from human want. But, in my early forties, I had managed to create a financial cushion that might be described as modest affluence.

I went to the NART "About Us" page. The offices were in Tysons Corner. Fifty staff. The CEO was named TJ Moncrieff. No information was given about Mr. Moncrieff, and there was little other information about the company.

I formulated a simple plan. I would visit NART Monday morning. I was familiar with the address. The building also housed on the last floor a club popular among the high tech community. I would try to see TJ Moncrieff. Start from the top. No calls, no appointments. Take advantage of the element of surprise. Ask him about the painting and the defacing.

For all its simplicity, of course, the plan also had the hallmarks of stupidity. It transcended not only the explicit limitations placed on me by X, but also the legal profession's bias in favor of inertia. My profession has its answer to the Hippocratic "first, do no harm." It is "when in doubt, do nothing." And yet there I was. I had become a reckless hunter after facts, the very kind of thing I had told X I did not do. And, at that, I had become more the clueless Inspector Clouseau than Sherlock Holmes or some equally ingenious sleuth.

But in my confused mind at the moment, there was nothing worse than to sit in my office, read about more deaths in Iraq, and await more sinister e-mails from little Marcel. The rash thing was the thing to do.

Monday was the deadline imposed by X for my final report. I opened my Outlook file and e-mailed him that I would need one more day, as I wanted to follow a last important lead. I hoped that he was occupied with one of his collecting interests that Sunday, and that I would not receive an answer in time enough to change my plan.

CHAPTER 15

▼

NART was the only tenant on the eighteenth floor of its building. The building's style, if style is the word for it, could be described as "law firm post-modern." The lobby was covered by speckled beige marble, making it look like an oversized bathroom. Office architecture has recently transitioned to this baroque minimalism. Tacking slabs of colored marble onto every surface achieves a dual goal. First, it gives the impression of prosperity, an impression essential to every business whose prosperity is either false or undeserved. Many businesses that have clients instead of customers fall into that category. Second, it does so without need for excessive adornments that would make the place look stuffy, according to the approximate aesthetics of tenants and visitors alike. The style is vulgar, but its vulgarity is thoroughly modern.

A guard compared me to my ID photo and let me go on without further ceremony. Most security personnel have the underappreciated tact to refrain from comment on the inevitable deterioration—more wrinkles, less hair—that time has wrought on the features of the traveler or visitor. The elevator was covered by marble too, making me wonder if its weight would allow it to ascend. It did, and regurgitated me into NART's offices. I walked out straight into a reception area and was immediately stunned. I was struck in the face, almost physically, by two things—the darkness and the silence.

The darkness was not total. Though the reception area was windowless, there were obviously sources of artificial light. There was none, however, sending diffuse light indiscriminately from the ceiling. And the total light available to the eyes was several notches below standard-intensity office building illumination. It is interesting how many unexamined choices underlie the conditions of our everyday environment, which we take for granted as inevitable.

But the silence was total. And I do not mean just the absence of sound—the calls, the voices, the shuffling feet, the Xeroxing. I mean also the absence of the sounds that we do not hear when they are present—the computers, the heating, the gurgle of Xerox machines just being ready to Xerox. Perhaps Marcel's famous cork-lined bedroom insulated its tormented tenant from all sounds just as effectively. Certainly, the otherworldly effect was studied. It made me fear that announcing myself to the receptionist would be regarded as a sacrilegious breach, like introducing oneself in church during Mass.

I nevertheless gave the receptionist—a man—my name and explained that I did not have an appointment, but would greatly appreciate a few minutes of Mr. Moncrieff's time on an important matter if he was available. If I breached a rule, the receptionist was clearly not charged with enforcing it. While he did not say I was expected, he certainly did not appear fazed by my lack of an appointment. Nor did he seem to communicate the fact of my presence to anyone by any visible means. Politely but wordlessly, he pointed me to a large sitting room integrated with the reception area, his slanted palm signaling I was to wait.

My eyes having gradually become accustomed to the low light, I could better observe my surroundings. They were the *crème de la crème* of the modernist canon. Form looked great looking functional everywhere. It was of course the ultra-expensive, touch-me-not kind of functionality. Soldiers resting on the ground near Baghdad, their head on their bag and feet on a tree trunk, and peasants doing the same in a field in Afghanistan, are often not knowledgeable about the modern decorative arts. They would be surprised to learn that their posture is the reconstituted inspiration for Charlotte Perriand's lounge chair. Such are the beginnings of these artifacts, which have in fact seldom been used in places where people fight or toil. They resemble in that respect cocktail-party Marxists. Prohibited, or at least frowned-upon, skin caressed my hand on the couch. Seal, or pony. And ornaments were completely absent.

Except for the art on the walls.

I knew, of course, that NART used to own *La Clepsydre*, but I was not prepared for the quantity and quality of its remaining corporate collection. Evidently, integrated optical solutions had escaped the dot-com crisis that accounted for the vacant commercial space throughout this high tech corridor. I could count perhaps twenty or more oils and watercolors hanging from the walls of the reception area alone. Spot lights tightly illuminated them without doing anything to defeat the surrounding darkness, giving the room a religious aura. They added to the contrast, literally night and day, between NART's abode and the secular vulgarity of its building. They reminded me of a Greek Orthodox church. The candles, lit by the faithful, heighten the sanctity of the austere icons in the temple's perpetual dusk, while the world outside is bathed in idolatrous light.

In fact, the 1937 Picasso must have been a somewhat discordant piece in this group. The focus seemed to be on early twentieth-century German and Austrian expressionism. I recognized the style of Beckmann, Nolde, Schiele. And, interspersed among the expressionists, there were a number of other figurative pictures that stood out stylistically. I saw two landscapes and a city square, all done in an assured but much more traditionalist hand. Unable to trace the style, I got up and walked to one of them. No signature.

I returned to the couch and started leafing through a solitary NART brochure lying on the Diego Giacometti that was doing duty as a coffee table. The usual stuff, new services inaugurated, new contracts announced. And then I came upon a spread of pictures from an art charity sponsored by NART, and spotted two people I knew. One was my client. The other was Christopher Nolan.

They stood facing the lens, a drink predictably ensconced in Nolan's right hand. They were both in tuxedoes, which had a different effect on each of them. In the case of X, the penguin black and white punctuated the red bulbous nose, but did not produce on his face the vulgar sense of occasion that often accompanies the attire. He was staring into the lens with his usual gruff intensity, as if he resented ceding control to the photographer. In the case of Nolan, on the other hand, the juxtaposition of disheveled head and black tie looked like the result of an artless photomontage. And in another contrast with X, Nolan was smiling beatifically. His features betrayed a state of exaltation. Evidently, his Marxist views and his sophistication took nothing away from the banal thrill of being around money and power.

While I knew both men, I had had no idea that they knew one another. My first thought was that they had both taken care to conceal that fact from me. Their acquaintance was certainly not something that X had volunteered when I had e-mailed him about my plan to show Andrée's portrait to Nolan. And Nolan, with his suspicious offhandedness, was likewise going on about the difficulty that I would have in gaining access to X. He had never suggested he could arrange an introduction himself.

But that was not all. I also wondered if X had told me the entire truth about NART. Did he know more about it than he had let on? He had mentioned NART only as the obscure prior owner of the painting, with whose identity I was not to trouble myself. And yet there he was attending NART's party.

What was going on? Was X in genuine need of my services? Or was I an unwitting pawn in a perverse game of chess he had devised?

I tried to comfort myself. X was a renowned patron of the arts. Very rich men photographed at art shows were almost an anthropological type. Nevertheless, the unexpected sight of the two unlikely cohorts, combined with the darkness and with the silent movie absurdity of the place, started to bring back the void in my stomach that had greeted little Marcel's last e-mail.

So here I was, in the heart of darkness. Was this the end of my journey through the jungle of vandalism and murder? Was I about to meet Kurtz, a crazed Marlon Brando embodying an unspeakable brutality?

Kurtz, or at least TJ Moncrieff, was a woman. A woman smoking a long pana-tela. She got up from her desk in the cavernous office to which I was finally led by another male assistant, presumably supplied by his employer with special noise-less soles. The room was as dark as the reception area. The difference was that there was an almost imperceptible oscillation, between dark and darker still, as if a candle was flickering somewhere. The walls were lined by more pictures by the German expressionists. I also spotted some more traditionalist watercolors, evi-dently in the hand of the same unknown master, as well as a full-length female nude.

The room was outlandishly cold. It wasn't just that the heat was off. With the thermometer at forty degrees outside, the air-conditioning was on.

But my hostess, once I was able to discern her well, was not the kind of woman who allows one's attention to stray for long to the things surrounding her, or even to inhuman temperatures. The wrinkles on her face and neck, unlifted and unbotoxed, suggested late fifties, perhaps sixty. But to call her beau-tiful would be meaningless.

When the Greeks dealt a setback to the powers of the Axis in 1940, pushing back the Duce's army to the Ionian Sea, Winston Churchill was ready with his customary *bon mot*. Until now we used to say Greeks fight like heroes. From now on we will say heroes fight like Greeks.

So it was with Ms. Moncrieff. She defined the concept. The primordial quid-dity of beauty had descended on her features. She reminded me of one of those famous beauties that we see in pictures from their youth many decades ago, a Diana Mosley or a Romy Schneider. We see them dressed in the now outmoded fashions of the day, or in period dress for the needs of a movie. We wonder what their contemporaries saw in them. We marvel at how the standards of beauty change from one generation to the next. And then we see a picture of the same woman, much older but in modern attire, and are stunned. We then conclude that these standards remain the same over time, but are disguised—in drag, as it were. The unchanging nature of beauty is veiled by the other norms of each age, the ones that do change.

In that Platonic view, too, we are probably wrong. Look no further than the Renoir nudes, vastly overrated as well as vastly overweight. But then Clemenceau, French prime minister during the First World War, already considered Renoir's women too fat. In beauty, as in many other things, the thesis of permanence and the antithesis of change are probably both necessary for understanding the concept. The more it changes, the more it stays the same.

But TJ's looks were above philosophy. Or they were all of philosophy at once. She was Plato's idea, Heracleitus' flowing river, Hegel's synthesis, Wittgenstein's gold meter, Gödel's undecidable proposition.

And it was not only the kind of beauty that defies age, but the kind that improves with it. The lines added knowledge to the perfection of the contours. The forty Shakespearean winters that besiege the brow had turned into sixty springs. Yes, Romy Schneider, had she lived to be sixty, would probably have looked like Ms. Moncrieff.

Her white hair was cut short. Her nose was French, slightly *retroussé*. Her huge green eyes were mesmerizing more for their passive being-there than for any penetrating gaze emanating from them—the defining characteristic shared by Andrée, Pablo, and Marcel. Indeed, in other ways too, TJ's looks seemed to be the opposite of Andrée's more ocean-bound beauty—darker complexion, Greek nose. Good to Andrée's evil? Evil to Andrée's good? They did share the sensual lips and prominent cheekbones—perhaps there was some Manichaean duality of good and bad in each of them. I was comforted briefly to think that Andrée, too, might still have looked beautiful at ninety-six. I was sure that Ms. Moncrieff would.

She wore no make-up and no jewels, in keeping with the no-ornaments rule of the house. Except for one blue stone, whose sparkle could only come from a diamond, set on a ring she wore on the middle finger of her left hand. It was so large and so brilliant that it resembled one of those gadgets with which Q endows James Bond, ready to pop open and emit a lethal blue laser beam. Her two-piece suit was a perfect match for the woman inside it and the priceless art around it. Dark blue, made by someone who had studied her figure well. The threads of its silk, perhaps woven by some cloned super-worm, practically crackled as she approached. There was no blouse under the vest that I could see.

It was only when I managed to extricate my eyes from her for a moment and survey the room more closely that I realized I had seen her before. The realization came compliments of the nude that I had caught a glimpse of when entering. It pictured an adolescent woman from the back, her face turned to the left in one-quarter profile. It was the same profile as that of my hostess—the callipygous woman on the canvas was Ms. Moncrieff. Younger by about four decades, her features were pretty but had not yet attained the polish that had been achieved at a more advanced age. There could nevertheless be no doubt about her identity. The young girl's face displayed an aggressive lack of self-consciousness about her nudity. It was the same confidence displayed in every lithe motion of my approaching hostess, albeit dressed now.

While the unabashed expression on the girl's face vaguely reminded me of something, I could not put my finger on it. It was her bare back that held the key. Not alabaster; marble. It was the back of the woman whom I had seen at the National Gallery. Ms. Moncrieff was the woman whose brunette companion had spurned so nonchalantly X's advances.

I was also able to make out the signature on the canvas. Leonor Fini. I knew from Nolan's onanism piece that the surrealist painter had been the fixture of many European playgrounds in her time. She would abandon surrealism for her own genre of sensual lesbianism whenever painting fetching women. Evidently, Ms. Moncrieff had been getting around when young. Perhaps the nude was another proof of Nolan's sexual frustration theory of creativity—an instance of Ms. Fini's unrequited appetites.

She left the cigar on an ashtray and offered her right hand, the other hand making a strange movement up to her neck. "Hello Mr. Melanchthon," she said. Her voice was the voice of a man, or perhaps a deep contralto. But its edge was also vaguely electronic, as if mixed by a hip-hop sound engineer at the studio. I realized that TJ's left hand was holding an electronic device to her vocal chords, damaged perhaps by an over-abundance of panatelas. So that was the content of the handbag with which she had been caressing her neck at the National Gallery. But strangely, her androgynous computer voice enhanced further her sensuality. Every Achilles needs a tendon to confirm his hero status. In TJ's case, the flaw not only confirmed her uniqueness, it also increased it. Her disability was like the lisp of a famous actress, which she has managed to convert from a liability to part of her legend.

"My name is TJ Moncrieff." the voice continued. "You can call me TJ. Or, if you prefer, Marcel."

I had obviously come to the right, or the wrong, place. In a flash, I remembered that I had seen a blue Italian roadster parked in the basement garage. It was the same car whose driver had given Superman a package outside the National

Gallery before speeding into the night. Ms. Moncrieff spared herself none of life's pleasures, including the boyish thrills of a fast car. Unless for her the thrill was associated with her modernist aesthetic. There is no human endeavor where form follows function more purely than the pursuit of acceleration.

"You clearly want an explanation, and I will supply one to you." I thought of the Wildean injunction, "Pray make it improbable." But there was little chance there was anything probable about TJ.

And she was not in a hurry. "Please, have a seat. Allow me to offer you a cigar," she said, opening the large humidor that kept her supply fresh. There was no point in refusing or rushing her. Time seemed to have stopped, or at least abnormally dilated, in this black hole of a place. I noticed that TJ was not wearing a watch, and none of the instruments that tell us the time were in evidence in her office. Except for an hourglass on her desk. Its sand, however, had trickled down its isthmus and settled in the lower compartment, seemingly at the beginning of time. I felt guilty for the ticks of my own watch. It would be difficult for me to try to impose any kind of rhythm on the interview. But I had to try.

The cigars in the humidor had no rings, like the unsigned pictures on the wall. But I had no doubt about their illegal provenance. TJ seemed to divine my thought.

"Our trade embargo laws do not apply to certain branches of the U.S. government."

The U.S. government. Fantastic. So, X's conspiracy dementia was not far off the mark after all. My queasiness returned. It only got worse when TJ picked a cigar for me and efficiently decapitated it with a guillotine-type cutter. The tool's evocative associations reminded me that my plan, like the administration's plans for Iraq, had not included an exit strategy. Hopefully, TJ's impending disclosures were consistent with my remaining alive after they were made.

But TJ was making no threats, at least not of the usual kind. "Allow me to light it up for you," she said, almost tenderly. She lit a long match. Standing in front of me, she leaned in until her face was a few centimeters from mine. Breaking off the tip of the match, then gently moving the burning remainder up and down the panatela, she went through a sensual ritual that seemed more like ultra-sophisticated torture in her hands.

She handed me the cigar. I took a puff. I sat paralyzed, but for my mouth struggling to inhale the smoke from the aged leaves. My senses were engulfed by her proximity. She seemed to disintegrate into a cubist collage of green eyes, silk over flesh, and faint wisp of perfume. I momentarily found it hard to compose her overwhelming proximity into a coherent whole. That siren's most lethal weapons were velvet, not steel. I tried to compose myself, summon up as much of my professional detachment as I could muster. I felt as if I was in court, steeling myself for the trickiest cross-examination of a witness in my career.

My cigar finally lit to her satisfaction, TJ settled on the couch beside me. She crossed her legs, and turned her speaking aid back on. She was ready to begin her story.

CHAPTER 16

▼

"Have you seen the film *Three Days of the Condor*, with Robert Redford and Fay Dunaway?" she started, not waiting for an answer. It was made in the mid-1970s. It was about a clandestine office set up by the CIA. A handful of operatives based in New York, with no formal links to the agency. But they did not do any of the usual spy things. Their mission was simply to read everything. They read novels, poetry, philosophy. They were supposed to identify anything of relevance to national security in the books they read, and report it to their bosses.

"The movie was more accurate than its makers thought. It was only a few years before that our office was created. In the late sixties. Our mission was art. But our mandate was broader than that of Robert Redford's character in the movie. We did not only have to identify the threat. We were charged with containing it."

"Is that why NART collects art? To contain it? How does selling *La Clepsydre* fit with the job?"

"*La Clepsydre* means hourglass, Mr. Melanchthon. It must take its time." She was pointing at her own inactive hourglass on her desk. "Please be patient. I first need to give you some background."

I sat back. This was not going to be the kind of cross-examination in which the artful lawyer leaves room only for a yes or no by the meek witness. Lawyers like this questioning, but not because it leads more efficiently to the truth. The origin of the technique has to do more with the lawyer's prevalent addiction—to the intoxicating sound of his own voice. This seemed one of the few vices not likely to be satisfied in this room. X, Nolan, TJ. The project was proving a good training exercise in listening.

"Not to bore you," TJ continued, "but art is individual expression. It is the apogee of the 'I.' But the state must suppress the I, like French epistolary rules. Every state must. Sure, democracies give their citizens rights. They give them constitutions, laws, the right to 'choose' their rulers every few years. But every one of these rights is also carefully circumscribed." Her right index finger drew a semi-circle around the cigar. "By the constitutions, by the laws, by the range of voters' choices. Democracy is a *table d'hôte* menu with two selections for each course. The one common characteristic of all inalienable rights is that they are alienable. And when it comes to a contest between the state and the individual, no ties are possible. The state must always win."

I had often heard speculation that the exorbitant amounts of money devoted to our intelligence gathering were not always spent with the utmost intelligence. But TJ's musings, if true, surpassed all rumors of bureaucratic waste. The taxpayers' money was being squandered on a beautiful woman's version of Political Science 101.

"The state does win, does it not?" I said. "Whoever has the weapons wins."

"Whoever *gets* the weapons does win. Bear with me, Mr. Melanchthon. I promise to make your visit worth your while."

Impossible to resist the lure of such a suggestive promise.

"There was a time when art used to have its limits too. For centuries it was financed by the church and the royal courts. And then the French revolution happened. Marat was murdered in his bathtub by his mistress. His crowd of dejected Jacobins shouted with one voice: Take up your brushes, David. Paint the gory scene. Do it for our cause. Revolutionary art was born. But it did not amount to much, not in the beginning. David's paintbrushes did nothing to stop *la terreur*. Goya did not hold back Napoleon Bonaparte. Byron wrote nice cadences, but could not prevent the fall of Mesolongi. The romantics, you see, may have chosen revolutionary themes, but that was all. They depicted the revolution but could not make it. They were still slaves to reason, even though they colored it in shades of pink.

"And then the real cracks started to show, I hardly need to tell you." A first nod by TJ that I was capable of knowledge, albeit of the kind open to every high-school student. "The impressionists defied the way things look. The cubists broke reality into pieces. By the twentieth century, all the checks were breaking down. All the little isms were besieging all the isms that matter."

"Which isms are the ones that matter?"

"The ones that pay me. The ones that pay you."

Having smoked one third of her cigar, TJ abandoned it and picked up another from the box—perhaps an aristocratic disdain for finishing food and drink, applied by analogy to her particular vice.

"The Nazis were the first to see the threat," she picked up again. "Joseph Goebbels was the first to recognize the subversive potential of the new art *and* do something about it."

Here were the Nazis, making their appearance. Was that the meaning of the swastika lovingly drawn by TJ in her last missive? A tribute to National Socialism's contribution to her capitalist specialty?

"But what did Joseph see?" she continued. She pronounced it "Yoseph," and talked about him in the cozy tones of friendship. Perhaps he had been her friend, if the reason his body could not be positively identified was somewhat different than the official version of incineration. For all I knew, he might have been more than a friend. According to the Nazi addict Nolan, Goebbels was one of the few undisputed heterosexuals in the upper ranks of the party.

"Joseph was a sensitive man. He saw the alienation of Beckmann's cityscapes, the sensual decadence of Schad's bohemians, the exaggerated suffering of Kathe Kollwitz's mothers. And he cringed. They were all about 'the poor I.' The new art was anathema to the Nazi philosophy—the Third Reich *über alles*."

"Mass murder takes a sensitive man to commit," I said.

"True," she agreed, disregarding my attempt at irony. "That is why mass murderers are men. They find comfort in numbers. Women are less sensitive. They can deal with solitary victims."

A dangerous theory in the mind of any woman alone with a man.

"But Joseph's achievement was not just to see the threat. After all, so had Plato, who would have ostracized artists from his Republic. And today, so can a moderately gifted elementary school boy." Even though she credited me with the potential for some knowledge, I had not yet graduated to junior high in my hostess's wise eyes.

"Plato taught, Goebbels did?" I interjected. "Was that his innovation? Making a teacher proud? I doubt Plato would have approved."

"No, Joseph's insight was more profound. In the threat, he saw a golden opportunity. The new art's methods opened wide vistas to him. Its illogic held the key to ultra-effective methods for suppressing the people—methods that had not been used with success since the Middle Ages. Methods like getting into people's dreams; talking directly to their subconscious; brainwashing them without involving their brain at all; stirring up the powers of superstition. In other words, what is today called marketing."

I thought of TJ's friend, the model, her brilliant nudity at the service of two investment bankers connected by an ampersand.

"Those were the lessons that art held for Joseph," TJ went on. "What is so devastating to some about Munch's screaming figure? That there is no reason for the scream. No explanation. No one even knows his, or her, sex. Joseph had the sensitivity to discern the power of an enlarged nose in a political caricature. He appreciated the wonders of film montage. He watched what the Bolsheviks were doing next door. The face of the evil capitalist alternates on the screen with the face of a fox. The spectator becomes a communist to the marrow. Who needs reasoned argument when he has Eisenstein at his service? Joseph the propagandist learned from Joseph the butcher."

Another "Yoseph." Meet Joseph Stalin, another good friend of mine.

"But, to be effective, the weapon must be kept secret. Because reason is still necessary as a pretext. The people must continue to think they are rational, even if they are driven by superstition. If I told you, Mr. Melanchthon, I would now like to hypnotize you, you would resist me, make my job more difficult."

I wondered whether I would truly resist such an attempt, even if I knew what she was up to. She seemed to be playing with me.

"So does that make art the state's ally?" I asked.

"It makes it the state's rape victim. Because the weapon can only be wielded by one. The state must have a monopoly over the magical powers unleashed by the new art. Enlarged noses can only be attached to Jewish faces in Nazi propaganda films.

"So this is what Joseph saw. And his innovation was that he stole modern art's thunder. He ridiculed it. He destroyed it when he could. When he could not, he expropriated it, aided by that discriminating collector, Hermann Göring. And he replaced it with Nazi art—the Aryan youths of Leni, the monuments of Speer. Nazi art was definitely an early form of NART."

"Is that NART's MO, too? Rape and pillage?"

"We did study their methods carefully. In fact"—a gesture of the cigar-holding hand sweeping the room—"most of the pictures you can see on the walls are from the degenerate art exhibition organized by Goebbels in 1937. Except, of course, for the Hitlers."

So that was the unidentified master.

"The Führer was a much more prolific painter than you may imagine," TJ continued. "The largest collector of his work is a Texan gentleman to whose house I would not care to be invited. The second largest collection belongs to the U.S. government. Curated by NART, and locked safely from public view. My bosses did not want his reputation as evil incarnate to be undermined by his artistic sensibilities. They didn't want his paintings to become fodder for some neo-Nazi character rehabilitation movement. I personally find his work crap, of course. But we felt we could not trust the taste of the general public."

TJ's confidence in her own aesthetic judgment was, by contrast, unshakeable. Well-deserved too, I was sure.

She paused. I turned to my right, toward the door, to take in one of the Führer's landscapes she had so mercilessly panned. As I did, I discovered the reason for the strange oscillation of the light in the office. Its source was two projectors lying on a low side table, which in turn stood by the wall facing TJ's desk. Each machine projected silent moving images in rapid succession on a small screen, fifteen by twenty inches. Each screen was surrounded by a gilded frame, as if the footage was a work of art of equal stature to the priceless canvases in the room.

It seemed to be Second World War documentary material. On the left hand screen, I saw the SS piling bodies in freshly dug graves. Then a beaming Churchill, cigar in hand, was making the victory sign. Then American GIs were lavishing cigarette packs like confetti upon exultant crowds. It was the same reception that we had hoped to receive in Iraq.

The other screen played a different movie. Hitler was receiving flowers from a young girl, giving her a pat and a smile. Enola Gay was hovering close to Hiroshima. A cloud had formed over Nagasaki. The familiar scenes were followed by one that I had never seen. Hitler appeared again. He was grayer than I ever remembered him being. His hair and moustache were almost white. He was kissing the ring of the Pope, surrounded by cardinals in the Vatican.

I turned to TJ. She was watching me watch, leaning back languidly, her legs crossed, a half-smile imprinted on her perfectly etched lips.

"Was he growing younger with age?" I asked.

"He certainly was growing less mature. But his hair was not turning darker. Both pieces were produced here," she explained with evident pride. "I call the one on the right *What If*. What if the Nazis had won, and lived to tell their story. I am particularly fond of the Führer's hair. It was easy enough, with some digital airbrushing. Quite the avuncular statesman, don't you think? All victors can afford to look kindly, no matter how monstrous. Stalin pulled it off. But the point is, any case can be made with quick splicing. Inspired editing could have made Nazis of all of us. I keep them playing all day. Each has one thousand hours' worth of material. They keep me on my toes. They remind me of the kind of power that we have to husband."

She was the consummate professional, like a lawyer playing continuing legal education tapes in his office.

"But, to return to our story, we easily concluded that the Nazis' methods were too blunt. In art, as in war, they went for the *blitzkrieg*. Their strategy was simply annihilate; steal the magic; then, create your own art. Destruction never works, however. It did not work then, it does not work now. Rudy Giuliani against Piss Christ. Jesse Helms against Mapplethorpe. These are battles that can never be won. And state art does not work either. Not in the heavy-handed ways the Nazis favored. If you want to glorify the Aryan race, singing paeans to it is not the way to go. In our view, more finesse was needed. A woman's touch."

"The kind of woman who prefers solitary victims? It might not be a very gentle touch."

She smiled.

"All women prefer solitary victims, Mr. Melanchthon. And the most lethal touch is gentle."

Velvet, not steel. TJ seemed to preach what she practiced.

"So we went to work. Our first coup came compliments of our most ancient allies, the French. A Frenchman wrote a book about how the New York school had stolen the idea of modern art from Paris in the fifties. One of his ideas was that the CIA had had a hand in the theft. Not true. But it inspired us.

"We liked the New York school because we loved abstraction. It was emasculated from the start. The message has no sting if there is no message, at least not one that can be deciphered. So we avidly financed all the abstract movements. Abstract expressionism? Minimalism? Conceptualism? You name it, we paid for it. Excrement in jars? Urine on canvas? Adorable. Makes such a statement. Please, Mr. Artist, eat, drink, produce some more. 'Revolutionary,' with the emphasis on the quotes. *Succès de scandale*, for a minute or two. But never a threat. Until it starts evoking a figure."

"How can you dictate a style?"

"NART dictates by suggesting. And by keeping mavericks in line. Take Philip Guston. When he abandoned abstraction to paint cartoons of Richard Nixon in the seventies, there was a chorus of disgust joined by all the priests of high art. The man had betrayed the purity of abstract expressionism, they cried in unison. I need hardly tell you who was holding the baton."

"What about still natures? Are they safe enough for NART? What about landscapes?"

"Don't underestimate the violence of nature, Mr. Melanchthon. Plus, you would be surprised what symbolisms left-wing critics can find in a bowl of lush red apples. No, only abstract art is truly safe. Except, of course, for art that has been commissioned by us. It is no coincidence that one of our age's most prominent collectors came up with the poster that defeated Labor in England in 1980. Long line of unemployed. Above it, the slogan: Labor is not working. And beneath, in almost invisible print: Vote for the Tories. A masterpiece. Art was again at the service of the ruling class, for the first time since the eighteenth century."

"A clever pun," I said. "But parties do not win elections on puns."

"What do they win them on? Their hundred-point covenants with the people? You see, Mr. Advocate, your job is to advocate. Well, I'm sorry to inform you, you no longer have a job. Not if the state has done its job. Not if we have done ours. You and your colleagues can only persuade the persuaded. You think that they have been convinced by your arguments. You are sure they have succumbed to your logic. You trumpet your success as an achievement of your fine legal mind. If they are especially gullible, they may think so too. But it is not so. They had already been convinced, most often by someone else's magic. It is the same magic that modern art conjured up and that the state stole. With the help of NART."

We were still getting nowhere. Minimalism. Philip Guston. The Tories. The futility of the legal profession. TJ's grand locutions. We were miles away from Pablo, Marcel, and murder. Murder other than mass murder, that is. The murder of a solitary victim.

"TJ," I pleaded, using her first name for the first time. "I don't claim to make magic. That's not my job. I make arguments. I would gladly cede all magic to NART."

But something was happening. I realized that my protest was growing weaker even as I was trying to articulate it. And I realized too that the smart-alecky remarks with which I had been interrupting my hostess were attempts to resist her fierce magnetic field.

I was slipping into a trance. Was it her mention of hypnosis? Could it be the cigar? I had read the CIA had tried to assassinate Fidel Castro by means of a cigar-bomb. Perhaps the failure of that brilliant plot had induced our spies to substitute hemlock for nitroglycerin?

Unlikely. I doubted that TJ would deign to resort to such artifices in her sorcery. It would be like a magician placing in his hat, in full sight of his audience, the rabbit that he plans to pull out of it. More likely, the reason was TJ's electronic monotone, given authority by her extraordinary beauty. It was as if the system itself had been talking in her computerized cadences. It was not that she made the system seem human. She made it seem perfect and therefore inhuman. The system was saying to me: I am so powerful because I am so beautiful. The victor's lullaby.

TJ too understood her growing influence on me. She didn't bother to ask for my patience this time. There was no need. I was not sure I wanted her to get to the point any more. My main worry now was that she might stop. Her explanation was becoming like Odysseus' return trip to Ithaca. It was more enchanting for the journey than for the destination.

CHAPTER 17

▼

"But all that was not enough." TJ appeared invigorated, like a vampire feeding off my growing inertia. A vampire. I had not thought of the lack of light in that light. But on that score, at least, I reassured myself. TJ's beauty was fresh, not vampiric. Her flesh was taut to the touch. Her eternal youth appeared to be the result of a more refined regimen than blood.

"For all our efforts, figures continued to creep up on modern canvases. More had to be done. We had to strike at the roots of the problem. We could not afford to contend ourselves with nurturing the conformists and making them appear revolutionary. We had to fight the true rebels.

"So I—we—had to come up with a new guiding principle." I could recognize the pride of maternity in the first person singular slip. Had TJ ever been a mother to corporeal children, I wondered. Or was she married to her crazy line of work?

"And we developed what I would describe as a three-step approach. First, discredit; second, embrace; third, castrate. Castrate by embracing, of course."

TJ seemed singularly capable of pulling off that third step. Perhaps the cigar-lighting ritual was a surrogate (or a portent?) for precisely such sweet emasculation.

"And we also had to triage. Notwithstanding our considerable resources, we could not hope to fight all of the art wars at once. The scattershot would dilute the bang. We had to concentrate on the greatest threats. Pablo was one. Marcel was another."

We were arriving at *terra firma*.

"Seems rather an arbitrary choice," I couldn't help saying.

"Every choice is a little arbitrary. But we had good reasons for narrowing the field. The question we put to ourselves was simple: Does it make people ungovernable?

"Take Pablo. The flag-bearer. The destroyer of reason. The surrealists followed, but they didn't have the discipline. Dali was an artistic suicide. He inflicted more ridicule on himself than Goebbels could have ever done. But Pablo went about creating his own worlds, governed by his own laws. It was subversive stuff. As I have said, modern government depends on the illusion of reason and the monopoly of magic. Breaking the spell is the worst thing an artist can do.

"Why does the state care about frontal profiles?" I asked. "Why are two eyes worse than one?"

"Two eyes are worse than one when they defy the laws of physics. Look at all statesmen-artists. Modern American presidents have happily refrained from adding artistic creation to their legacy. The public is more comfortable with them holding golf clubs than paint brushes. European statesmen are more adventurous. Hitler was not the only painter. Think of Churchill's watercolors. I have always wanted to sponsor one day a comparative retrospective of the two men's work. Adolph versus Winston: war on canvas. But the point is, can you imagine any of these powerful men painting frontal profiles? Putting an eye where the ear should be? Even if they had, their spokesmen would have denied it more forcefully than they deny reports of war atrocities. Government does not like to commit suicide.

"Plus, Pablo disdained abstraction. In all his life, he never did one abstract canvas. Often hard to tell, but the shape of things was always there."

"Disdained abstraction." I remembered that X had used the same phrase. Had he been the recipient of the same dissertation? TJ's eager pupil?

"Hitler disdained abstraction too, to judge from these watercolors," I said. And the nude hanging from the wall is thankfully an excellent likeness." Was I flirting with her? "Why would it be a capital crime for Pablo?"

"That's very kind of you, Mr. Melanchthon. Unfortunately, the better the likeness, the heavier the burden on the subject. But Pablo did not go for excellent likeness. And this was not his only crime.

"Most important, there was Pablo's politics. Little protests at first, newspaper war stories jumping out of the collages. Then, anti-Franco cartoons. Then, of course, there was *Guernica*. One of our worst headaches. As they say in writing classes, show, don't tell. One eye/tear, one screaming mouth, worth all the anti-war manifestos that could be written.

"What really happened in Guernica? Who knows? Where is it? Who cares? Hardly anyone remembers that the real name of the city in Basque is Gernika.

Right-wing historians have downplayed the bombing, you know. A minor incident, they say. A misfiring. Göring's airplanes were intended to bomb military
positions of the Republican army. No more than ninety civilians were killed.
Most of the damage was done by gas tank ambushes laid by the guerillas anyway.
What is the historical truth? It doesn't matter. Pablo's art has obliterated the significance of facts. *Guernica* was the best piece of propaganda the world had ever
seen. NART would not be worth its salt if we did not take action."

"So what action *did* you take?"

"First, we discredited. Pablo's life, his defiance of convention, became our
weapons. Left-wing, a card-carrying member of the French communist party,
with an ax to grind against the system. A Marxist who did not live as he
preached—why, didn't he stay at the Savoy when in London? And a womanizing
Marxist to boot—a strange short satyr going around naked. And what about that,
what about his famed virility? Was it the real thing, or another figment of his
fecund imagination? Why did he need his women convoluted in cubist triangles?
Did a real woman's curves not do it for him?"

"Are you challenging the man's virility? Must be a hard sell even for you."

"It takes a woman to challenge a great man's virility. In fact, it was easy to
place some carefully worded passages, to insinuate some rumor in the mind of an
ambitious biographer or two. We have always found that young writers trying to
create a name for themselves are eager to receive NART's grants.

"Take Christopher Nolan. I gather you know him. An opinionated man,
wouldn't you say? And yet you would be surprised how malleable his views can
be. Not procreate, create. An original theory, to be sure. Originating in this
office. Do you think he came up with his ingenious speculation about the great
man's impotence? He did a good job writing it up. But NART whispered it in his
ear."

I had a good idea who had done the actual whispering. Did TJ need her
machine to whisper as well as talk? I couldn't resist the vision of my hostess sitting down with a subdued Nolan on the sofa where we now sat. She would touch
him lightly. She would envelop him with the same sensual aura that now sur-
feited my senses. Her light aroma would deliver to his nostrils promises that were
irresistible even though both of them knew they would not be kept. Since the
beginning of recorded history, it has taken such unspoken inducements to reduce
the most loquacious men to lifeless putty in a woman's hands.

"Second, we embraced. The idea was to pour millions into the Picasso market.
It initially caused some heartache to our bean-counting masters. I had to marshal
all my powers of persuasion to make them think it through."

I could attest these powers were considerable, and I had to restrain myself from imagining exactly how they had been deployed. Certainly, reasoned argument would not have been part of her strategy.

"Who signed the checks?" I asked.

"Not me. I do not own a checkbook. But since the 1970s, NART has financed many of the winning bids for important Picasso works. Surrogates have placed the bids. Anonymous collectors, whose identity we were happy to leave to the art world's gossip and the imagination of the crowds."

I thought of my own fascination with the unnamed collecting demigods. My disappointment at meeting someone like X and realizing he was mortal was one thing. The knowledge they may have been NART's pawns was quite another, even more effective at cutting them down to size. X, too? I wondered.

"You know the results. Prices have been going nowhere but up. One million, five million, ten million. One hundred million. Never enough. The hammer of the auctioneer was music to our ears.

"And it paid. The Marxist's work became the most capitalist of hard currencies. The ultimate status symbol. A materialist aspiration is no longer a threat. It is hard to stage a revolution when you are hanging from a Park Avenue wall. Net-net? Total victory." New cigar, triumphant click of the guillotine. "Total castration."

"So everything has its price," I offered rather lamely. "Even revolution has its price."

"*Merchandise* has its price," TJ corrected. "Pablo's art was always for sale. He wanted to have it both ways. If you can create wealth every day with your bare hands, it's easy to be against ownership. Until you create so much wealth that you become your own collector. That's what he liked to say, you know. That he has the best Picasso collection in the world. He could be a little smug. His pride helped us raise his price. So did his death. I know of very few Marxist estates. And of very few virile corpses."

"So are you saying the U.S. government owns a slew of Picassos? Where are they? In a vault?"

"Why shouldn't it? It owns nuclear weapons. Where are *they*? The U.S. government owns more things than you imagine. Perhaps not as many as the Vatican."

"Sounds like a luxurious strategy." I was struggling to make my contributions not sound completely foolish.

"Luxury is a NART specialty. The most expensive things have always been chosen by women and paid for by men. Neither feminism nor Marxism can change this. I myself have always been pro-choice. Woman's choice. Plus, I have never understood cost-cutting. Efficiency in my job is a waste."

"And what is waste?"

"A necessity. But we didn't just throw money at the problem. We did other things too over the years, up until today. Little things that people do not notice but that add up. When the state secretary gave a press conference after his remarks at the UN last year, it was we who spotted the risk from the *Guernica* tapestry hanging in the corridor outside the Security Council chamber. Unseemly to talk about war against its backdrop. Cabinet secretaries and their staffs are not sensitive to such things. We had to go through endless days of bureaucratic squabbling to get it covered by a shroud. A *New York Times* columnist got it, as she often does.

"And you must have thought X crazy for seeing some sinister connection in Chairman Lower's Picassoesque remark. I know, he told me. You were wrong. A helpful suggestion to the chairman's office on our part."

"So what *is* X's role?" I could not resist asking, mystified by what game my client was playing. The man who was paying me to unlock the great mystery was gossiping about my project with the woman who held the key. "What side is he on?"

She laughed. It was strangely a xylophone laugh, as if a different octave on her machine had been enlisted to mark the change of mood. "What do you think? X has all the money, all the power. He is on both sides."

As in the Leonard Cohen song, I thought: "Jazz police is paid by J. Paul Getty, jazz is paid by J. Paul Getty too." X paid for the art. And he also paid for NART.

"But Marcel was a more difficult problem. He was an insider, you see. Upper bourgeoisie, with burning social-climbing ambition. Clearly establishment material. He did not need to be hung in salons, he avidly frequented them. And his insiderdom made him more corrosive. An insidious virus to Pablo's more easily curable influenza. Impossible to discount him as a disgruntled subversive."

"But he was not entirely gruntled either, was he?"

"He was unhappy. And he *was* subversive. Marcel's message was futility. Life is a tragedy. Habit makes us into automatons, and there is no way to escape its claws. Reason? Hopeless. Doesn't help us understand one thing. The only thing to hope for is the little ridiculous incidents that awaken us to the reality of the past, without any ability on our part to precipitate them. The only paradise is the one we have lost."

"Is NART pro-paradise, too?" So far, NART seemed more of a hell partisan to me.

"No. We only believe in the faith in it. But if it is hard to govern fans of cubism, it is impossible to govern people so thoroughly disillusioned. The system needs people to be slaves to habit and to reason. And it needs them not to know it. You think that religion is the opium of the people? Marx didn't have his drugs straight. *Reason* is the opium that numbs the people. The church and the state come afterwards with their hallucinogenics as the chaser. Their LSD can then do its job without inhibitions. The sleepwalkers do what the system wants them to do. Why do you think democracies prohibit drinking on Election Day? To ensure the voters make a rational choice? No one who matters wants the voters to make rational choices. The system distrusts alcohol for the same reason it distrusts art. It wants to control exclusively the voters' stimulants. Religion, patriotism, family values, human rights. Whatever the propaganda machine has chosen for its subliminal persuasion. But reason must be the enabling narcotic."

"I don't think therefore I am? Is that NART's philosophy?"

"I don't think therefore I don't matter would be closer. So. The determination was made at the highest quarters," TJ continued, pointing her finger up toward the ceiling. "We need reason. We need habit. And we must strike at anyone who exposes them."

The highest quarters: who on earth did TJ mean? The president? I wondered if any president had made his way through *La Recherche*. Perhaps after they left office. Perhaps Calvin Coolidge, he seemed to have free time. Perhaps Bill Clinton.

Again she was ahead of me. "You are too much enthralled with your laws, Mr. Attorney-at-law," she said, a palpable combination of scorn and bitterness in her voice. "The president, the Supreme Court, the Congress. They are all incidental, part of your democratic fictions. Holding onto power is a more serious matter. And it is not done with memos, meetings, or chains of command. Winks, nods, snubs and shrugs. That's what it takes. It's a cold business."

It was the first time TJ was displaying emotion. Even the computerized edge of her voice was registering some electronic sadness, as if the system itself was feeling a little melancholy about doing what was necessary.

"But back to Marcel," she regrouped. "He was surely not the only one, there were other despair propagandists. But they were easier to dispose of. Heidegger, we could brand a Nazi. Sartre, a Marxist. And they did not write novels, or at least not very good ones. So there was our problem, how to deal with Marcel's little great masterpiece."

"Couldn't you pan it? Say the sentences are too long?"

"We did. But there is only so much righteous indignation you can hang on syntax. Our solution you must have guessed by now: cultivate the myth of his homosexuality. We did not invent it, I am sorry to say. But it was there to be exploited."

"Who did invent it?"

"Others did," TJ said cryptically. "Really, the myth begged to be invented. It was Marcel's fault."

"For being effeminate?"

"For being good. We live, as you may have noticed, Mr. Melanchthon, in an age of over-excitement. We see skill, and we rush to call it talent. We see talent, and we proclaim it genius. But Marcel was the real thing. And his genius was to make his 'I' into our 'I.' We read these long sentences and realize we are staring at a mirror—an X-ray, magnifying glass mirror. We see things so private that we never suspected anyone else of having experienced them. Our tiniest quirks become enlarged one million times under the microscope of his owlish eyes. What we thought eccentric is shown to be common currency, like the dollar or the kilogram."

"Was that his fault? Empathy? Is empathy effeminate?"

"I don't know. If it's feminine, I have never felt it. But the message becomes less universal if its sender is a queer who enjoyed watching rats being tortured. A tall tale, by the way. Check Painter's evidence—all rumor. And notice the big assumption—that preoccupation with rats is a sign of homosexual desire. Who has established such a curious fact?"

"I'm not an expert on homosexual preferences," I said.

"Of course you are not," she smiled. Was she challenging my virility too? Was I a member of the same elite club as Pablo Picasso?

"And you would not be caught dead possessing such expertise, would you? This is the point. It is easier to discredit a man who had to turn his boyfriend into a woman to appear 'normal.' A minute ago, you thought 'this could be me.' Then you ponder this neurotic deviant trying to look like you, and the antidote sets in. 'What's wrong with me?' you ask yourself. For all the achievements of the gay rights movement, we have found that we could always rely on one atavistic fear of the heterosexual male. We could count on man's paranoia about identifying with someone who likes being penetrated. It also accounts for men shirking women's books. Chick lit is for chicks, no?

"We would have promoted the idea even if it had been true, of course. But it was not. Marcel may have had homosexual tendencies. He may even have been bisexual. Everyone is, more or less, with the possible exception of Adam and Eve. But Marcel liked women. And he loved Andrée Duplessis."

The electronic aid's voice broke at the last sentence. Perhaps a drop of saliva, nectar from TJ's mouth, made it crackle. It reminded me of the high notes Paul's voice had broken into when he was announcing the same discovery.

And then I froze at the thought.

CHAPTER 18

▼

The same discovery. TJ was telling me exactly the same story that Paul had struggled to piece together from mountains of print, based on the little clues that she had provided us. Marcel was not really gay. He was in love with Andrée.

It was too neat. It was like two jigsaw puzzle pieces that fit exactly together even though they belong to different jigsaw puzzles.

Had NART bugged my office? Had TJ been eavesdropping on my conversations with my colleague? Had she read the draft memo to X? Had she staged this interview to dispel all my doubts about the extravagant yarn she had been pushing on Paul and me from the start? The doubts began to grow again. But my dazed mind could not give them a more concrete form.

"You know much of the rest," TJ continued. Her certainty that I knew did nothing to allay my concerns. What about the muscular woman jogger whom I had so wrongly suspected of being a sniper in place of the squirrel? Was she a spy after all? TJ's employee?

My hostess, by contrast, seemed to be growing more relaxed. She settled back on the sofa. Her cigar of the moment had a longer pillar of ash on its end than its predecessors. No jerky dispensing of the ashes on the ashtray for a seasoned cigar smoker like TJ.

"Who could know that Pablo was haunted by the strange couple with eyes like his that he had met at the beach in Cabourg years ago?" She asked herself. "And then, right after he painted *Guernica*, Pablo decided to decipher the riddle of Albertine for posterity. When we discovered the painting, we found ourselves faced with a crisis that would test our organization's mettle."

"How did you discover the painting?"

"We have our sources." Evasive again. "It doesn't really matter. Our two biggest problems had combined. The *Guernica* eye/tear was being shed over the inexorable loss of time."

"So which is it, an eye or a tear?"

"It is the eye's last tear. Nolan may have boasted to you that all the scholars have misinterpreted the last sketch for *Guernica*. He likes to say they have missed the reason why Picasso erased the actual tear running from the hurrying woman's eye. He's right about the reason, but not because it is so obvious to his expert eyes. I told him. And Pablo told me."

TJ had really been getting around in her youth.

"Pablo was right. Removing the tear made the eyes streaming down the other faces more powerful. And now here was another one, distorting Andrée's beautiful face. The horror of war threatened to turn into total dread at man's existence. It was as if the two most potent isotopes were interacting to create a hydrogen bomb, capable of blowing the entire system up into a mushroom cloud."

"It doesn't sound very chemically correct."

"*Alchemy* is our specialty. By contrast, destruction was never our thing. But extraordinary measures were called for. What would you have done? Wouldn't you have chosen to avert a nuclear detonation by painting over a few square inches of canvas? For us, it was a no-brainer."

"But you did more, didn't you?"

After drawing an unprecedented fifth puff on her cigar, TJ put it down. I noticed that the exertion of exegesis had now made her breathing a little heavier, a drum-n-bass accompaniment to the hip-hop contralto. But she had lost none of her poise.

"You mean did we have Andrée killed? We did. Correct me if I am wrong, but I imagine you subscribe to a morality code that regards murder as more reprehensible than vandalism. NART does not. But it doesn't matter. There too, I am afraid we had little choice."

TJ picked up a crumpled piece of paper lying on the coffee table and handed it to me. It was a short handwritten note, in French. It was a love note. But it was written in the careful calligraphy of a letter that is intended to be read not just by the lover.

Mon chéri Marcel

Tu as su toujours se faire aimer, et tu n'as su jamais se faire oublier. On a perdu tellement de temps.

Ton Andrée

"'My darling Marcel,'" TJ translated for me, her voice all quotes. "'You always knew to make yourself loved, and you never knew to make yourself forgotten. We lost so much time. Your Andrée.' Pathetic, isn't it, coming from a ninety-six-year-old woman. Our little Andrée would have put her note in her will papers. She would have outed herself, and us, for posterity. She would have achieved the feat that we had prevented Pablo from accomplishing twenty-five years before. A senile whim would have jeopardized the hard work of decades. It was not a difficult decision either. As Stalin would have said, 'No woman, no problem.'"

But the unapologetic defense was now barely registering, as if my mind had turned down the volume of TJ's monotone. Because I remembered one of the passages from *La Recherche* that I had gone back to read the day before. It was the one paragraph in the thousands of pages where the narrator reveals his name. He drops the mask of the universal I and affords a glimpse of the suffering man behind. And it is the memory of Albertine that does it. The narrator's love for her makes him drop all pretense. He puts in Albertine's mouth her actual words of love exactly as she had spoken them. When waking up in my room, he says, she would whisper to me "my darling," followed by my Christian name. Assuming, he continues, that the narrator had the same name as the writer of this book, that would be: "My darling Marcel."

I am not an instinctive man. When I have a bad dream, I manage to comfort myself by remembering my complete lack of a sixth sense. But some infallible instinct must have awakened from its hibernation inside my unconscious. It spoke with an authority that neither logic nor TJ's stories could have produced. It told me that the "darling Marcel" reaching me from Andrée Duplessis's grave and Albertine's immortalized sweet nothings were uttered by the same woman. Suddenly, all my doubts evaporated. Andrée was Albertine, and she died for it.

Suddenly. And perhaps, stupidly.

"Are you a romantic, Mr. Melanchthon?" My omniscient hostess scoffed. "Don't be. You are a lawyer. It would be more fitting if you tried to judge me instead. But you must not do that either. I probably should tell you one more thing. Not very important in the scheme of things. I said that we had Andrée killed. It would be more precise to say that I killed her. Single-handedly, no surrogates this time. And no regrets. You see, I knew Andrée."

TJ's voice had become deeper, and almost entirely metallic now.

"We met in Cabourg in the 1950s. I was a teenager, spending the summer with my parents. Andrée was in her still alluring fifties, visiting her old haunts. She told me about Marcel. She introduced me to Pablo. She also introduced me to Gomorrah. And then the summer passed, and she left me. I don't remember in which order. I was no match for the man with the owl's eyes. I am not talking about jealousy, you understand. It was more one of those cases where you are reassured by some information you have collected at one place or another. It helps confirm you are doing the right thing."

So the French, and Paul, were right. *Cherchez la femme.* It would have provided the key. I imagined the fifty-something woman and the eighteen-year-old girl playing on the sand in Cabourg. I saw the older woman's exacting tongue explore languidly the inexperienced mouth, titillate the pink nipples into erection. And I understood for a moment what Marcel had felt—jealousy mixed with arousal. Then I imagined the two women locked in their final, lethal embrace decades later.

So my dream of the young drowning Amazon and the impassive mother was connected to work after all, except the woman was not the girl's mother. She was not anyone's mother.

For a moment I was paralyzed by fear. What Manchurian-candidate methods had TJ employed to get inside my head? When she joked about hypnotizing me, was she joking? Was hypnosis truly part of NART's formidable arsenal?

I also realized what bell had been rung in my mind by the young TJ's look in the Fini portrait. The aggressive lack of shame in her nudity had sired offspring. It had bred the defiance of her young model friend, equally naked, in the investment bank ad. Like a sinister Pygmalion, TJ was molding her lover to be young TJ to her Andrée. I did not envy the beautiful model. Her fate was sealed. She was going to become brokenhearted with mathematical certainty, as her tormentor had been before mastering the instruments of torture.

My hostess, for her part, continued to radiate her Olympian calm. Amazons cut off their right breast for the sake of their archery. This Penthesilea's breasts were intact, still stretching the blue silk of her jacket at the age of sixty. But other organs had suffered. To practice her own martial art uninhibited, TJ seemed to have commissioned a heart transplant procedure that allowed ice water to course through her veins.

Something made me turn to my right, toward the door. There was someone else in the room.

CHAPTER 19

▼

It was another man at TJ's service, who had entered her office as noiselessly as his predecessor. A mustachioed, white-gloved waiter, carrying a silver tray with two tiny coffee cups. With completely fluid motion, he deposited them on the low table between us. He bowed with the self-effacing modesty of a bow that does not ask to be acknowledged, and disappeared.

"Turkish," TJ said. "No sugar. Only the dregs. As you like it."

She remained solicitous of my tastes. And eerily knowledgeable about them.

But thanks to the interruption, however unobtrusive, and the first sips of the strong coffee, something happened. Slowly, the sweet hemlock supplied by TJ's soliloquies started to wear off. Logic started again to seep into my numbed senses.

"Find out the why," X had instructed me. "The who will flow from the why." I had achieved the reverse. I knew the who, or so I thought. But the why didn't make sense. In fact, the more TJ explained, the less sense it made.

OK, this was not the case of a private vendetta. To be sure, glaciers can unleash more fury than volcanoes. I was nevertheless ready to accept TJ's claim that Andrée's mistreatment of her young pupil had only helped the pupil do "the right thing" decades later. That it was not the decisive factor. But the right thing was murder. To hear TJ, the formidable machinery of the state had been mobilized to commit it. Over what? A painting? A love note? Andrée had died for being Albertine? Why?

"I don't buy it," I said, raising my voice in an effort to shake myself completely from the trance. Guilt immediately overtook me. I felt like a suicidal lawyer asked a question by the Chief Justice during oral argument in the Supreme Court. A couple of seconds tick away, and the lawyer is as stunned as the audience when he hears himself say: "Don't be stupid." Irreverence can be almost as sacrilegious when it is directed to Satan as to God. But, sacrilege aside, I had to soldier on. Let Satan be damned.

"I don't buy it. The two most potent isotopes. Nuclear detonation. Mushroom cloud. Why? Because a painter painted the portrait of a woman? Because the woman had been the girlfriend of a writer who was not really homosexual? It doesn't appear too much of a nuclear explosion to me."

"You are so logical. You do do justice to your profession."

"Do do." There was not a wide range of emotions that TJ needed her electronic voice product to express. But she had certainly picked her voice aid to be capable of the modulations required for sarcasm.

"Well, Mr. Logician, turn the love note over."

I did. The love note was scribbled on the back of a document in memo format. It was typed on an old typewriter, whose characters had evidently been worn to different degrees, creating a dizzying impression of unevenness on the paper. Stamps of officialdom danced before my eyes. Special Branch of something. Special Branch of U.S. something. Classified. Secret. A place and a date: Munich, September 30, 1938. A familiar name on the "From" line: TJ Moncrieff. How old could my hostess be? Was she really the devil? No recipient name. On the "Re" line: "The War of Art."

I looked further down. Four words, in two couplets:

Pablo Red
Marcel Queer

Then a question and an answer: "Half-Jewish? That I doubt we could use Stateside." And finally, a sentence: "Many in Washington, art lovers all, would probably side with H in this particular purge."

"My parents gave me my father's name," TJ said. "TJ Moncrieff was a dashing man. He worked for the U.S. government. A small organization, predecessor of the OSS. He was friends with Lindbergh. And he was friends with Goebbels. He never really idolized Hitler. He was the kind of man who preferred to *be* idolized. But he certainly sympathized with him."

Hitler again. Goebbels again.

"When Lindbergh visited Germany, Dad was with him. He was also in Munich when Chamberlain appeased the Führer. Dad didn't need to do any appeasing. He and Joseph got along famously. But if appeasement is a bad word, Dad did worse. He forged a secret pact with Joseph. A U.S.-German pact. Psychological operations. Propaganda. They called it 'The War of Art.' And, like people in his era, he was naïve enough to believe that words on paper could remain secret. Remember, this was in the days before a tap on the keyboard could spread a secret to millions. But he didn't count on a perfidious daughter, who would find the memo in his papers, and give it to her lover."

"You gave it to Andrée? Why?"

"There is a scene in *La Recherche* in which the daughter of Vinteuil, the composer, is told by her lesbian lover to desecrate her father's picture."

That was the sadomasochistic scene that Paul had talked to me about. Another uncanny coincidence.

"Andrée was obsessed with that scene. She said to me that all young women must betray their father for their lover. She thought it was a rite of passage. She commanded me to betray mine. I did. I did, even though I worshipped my father, you know. So there, do you have your explanation?"

"It's still improbable."

"Probabilities seldom interfere with our life. Accidents usually do. You say the great painter's portrait of a woman is no big deal. You say, if the woman was the great queer's girlfriend, so what? I disagree. These no big deals and these so whats are what propaganda is all about. They are certainly what NART is all about. People don't think big thoughts. They think small assumptions. Upset them, and anything can happen.

"But OK," she continued. "I grant you that perhaps NART's thinking is a little outside the mainstream of the U.S. government's views on that subject. This has been mentioned to me before. You are not the first logician to set foot in this office, you know. But if the dirty little secret of Marcel's normalcy was not enough for some of our masters, what is on the back of the love note was enough for all of them. Would be enough even for you, *Monsieur l' Avocat*. A maverick special branch of the U.S. government collaborated with the Nazi propaganda machine to create myths. I said we improved their methods. What I didn't say was that we used their ideas. TJ Moncrieff used them in the thirties. Another TJ Moncrieff revived them decades later. And as you would say in your profession, there was a smoking gun document to prove it. There is your nuclear explosion right there. There are some truths that no one can afford. Not even the U.S. government."

CHAPTER 20

▼

So that was why. I felt I knew as much of that why as I would ever learn. But I still didn't know the ultimate why. No story is about facts; all stories are about motive, I had been counseled by one of my litigation partners. Why had TJ decided to blow the whistle on her bosses and herself? Why had she become little Marcel? Why had she told me her story?

Was it to take her crimes off her chest? Unlikely. First of all, I was an improbable fountain of solace. I doubted that a woman of TJ's impossibly discriminating standards had discerned in me reserves of spirituality I had never known existed. She viewed me as a hapless lawyer who needs all the help he can get, and not unjustly. But most important, to hear her account, TJ's conscience remained profoundly untroubled. Why then had she decided to confess dark secrets that evidently didn't prevent her from sleeping the sleep of the just? And why had she chosen me as her confessor?

This time TJ remained silent, refraining from her customary mind-reading. So I asked her why.

For the first time, she missed one or two beats, as though collecting her thoughts. But when she spoke, there was no hesitation in the electronic voice.

"It was in part a lobbying tactic. I think you know Washington enough to know this: power can never be undone by any external force. It can only be undone by its own undoing. Civil war. Internecine strife. Turf battles. The victors' fight over the spoils.

"The intelligence community is no different. And our battles have to be waged with one hand tied behind our backs. You see, spies must keep secrets. They cannot give their masters the commodity that the masters value the most—credit.

So, success breeds envy. Envy breeds bureaucratic death—a form of demise known by more euphemisms than the real thing. Budgetary adjustment. Reprioritization. Devolution. Other claims on the black-box money become more urgent.

"The war in Iraq, for example. Who needs to continue fighting art when we must find a reason for fighting a real war? Why are you striking at imaginary windmills when we must locate weapons of mass destruction—yesterday? You have been successful, you say. Brava. Let's declare victory on art and move on. You would like to buy another Picasso? Do you know how many spies on the ground that money can buy us? And your Picasso, how many battalions does he command? Questions become more and more difficult to answer when the questioning grows louder.

"Some deftness was needed. Would it hurt our cause—NART's cause—if a leak could showcase the importance of our work? A hint to a man like X, aided by his capable counsel. What if the cocktail of Pablo and Marcel were shown to be the nuclear threat that it is? Would our masters continue to care exclusively about nickel-and-dime rockets and wooden surveillance drones in Iraq?

"This is how you came in, Mr. Melanchthon. Did you think my motives were any nobler? Well, they were not. Did you hope your role was more chivalrous? It wasn't. The war? A silly distraction, a vexing risk for my budget, nothing worse. I did watch the footage on *CNN*, as I know you have done. And I also watched *Al Jazeera*. I don't know Arabic, but I always watch on mute anyway. It allows you to focus on the images. Every evening I watched the Iraqi women mourning in their black scarves. They always wore black, even with the dead fresh at their feet—always prepared for tragedy. One had a dead baby in her arms. She looked strikingly like the mother on the left panel of *Guernica*. Her face was eclipsed by the same silent wail. But my interest was only aesthetic, professional. You…on the other hand. Would I be wrong in guessing that you, Mr. Melanchthon, would have indulged a more…emotional reaction? You are such an incurable romantic. Such a…pacifist."

Despite the newly halting speech, her sarcasm continued to drip unabated. But quite abruptly, something had changed.

TJ looked older now. The green light reposing in her eyes had dimmed, sinking the room into even greater darkness. Her posture had sagged. Her DNA appeared to have misplaced the proud way in which she carried her head and projected her chest. The change was slight, but its effect was devastating. She reminded me of a supermodel breezing down the runway at a fashion show. She stumbles on her high heels right before turning, and falls. Her looks are unscathed, but the poise that elevated them to superhuman proportions is gone. She becomes a rabbit frightened in the glare of the same camera lights that were intended to immortalize her.

So TJ's beauty was not invincible after all. It had collided with a mysterious immovable object. Was it, despite her protestations, the violence of war? She certainly looked violated. A similar effect would have been produced if her girlfriend's nude photo from the investment bank poster had been despoiled by a crude joke. I imagined the perfect figure of TJ's lover cut out of the photo and glued in another one, against the backdrop of an Iraqi jail. A cretinous woman in khakis gives her nudity a grotesque thumbs-up in the foreground.

Or was time a more likely perpetrator than war? An absent-minded professor, he had remembered suddenly the job he had long neglected—weathering TJ's youth. Or a bargain had been unwound, and the Leonor Fini portrait of the adolescent TJ had lost its magic faculties of keeping its subject young. With overcompensating force, time had invaded, taking the room by storm and introducing my hostess to the facts of decay. I thought of the murals in Roman catacombs. Having survived intact for millennia, they disintegrate in one second before the eyes of the subway construction crew. The holes opened by the drills expose them to the polluted air from which they had been sheltered.

And she, the androgynous soldier hardened by so many battles, now seemed fragile. The Superwoman who knows no remorse looked in need of the solace that she had made such a point of defying. The wrinkles lining her brow and surrounding her eyes were now the dominant feature on her face.

I put my hand on the small of her back. She didn't pull back. I leaned closer, and took her speaking device away from her with my other hand. She didn't resist. I whispered in her ear the favor that I wanted from her. She remained motionless.

I looked at the two framed screens. The black and white light from the competing mockumentaries still flickered on them. Churchill and Hitler were both painting, each doing battle with an easel in the same bucolic setting. Each had an angelic little boy lolling by his side—one of them looked faintly like a young Paul. The airbrushed Führer was now sporting a bushier white moustache. A beret, no doubt presented to him by a doting French subject, added bohemian insouciance to his look. A kindly-looking Goebbels, his angular face smoothed by a well-groomed beard, hovered nearby. He looked like a thin and short Santa Claus.

I walked over and turned off the two projectors, each tape snapping back around its cartridge. Then I walked to TJ's desk, stood the hourglass on the other end, and got out quickly as the sand started trickling down.

CHAPTER 21

▼

There was a lot to do in the office on Tuesday morning. First, finally, I had to complete the memo to X. Professional, privileged, highly confidential. Just the facts. He probably knew most of them anyway. Then, a bouquet of orchids had to be ordered for TJ. Ancient Greeks prized hospitality above all virtues, and its bonds excused all crime. Whatever else she was, TJ had been an exquisite hostess to me. I chose the number ninety-six, though. I shared the European bemusement at Americans' dozens of roses. But even numbers are acceptable beyond fifty, even under European etiquette. I wondered if she would count them. She probably would not need to.

Then, a few minutes before eleven, I went to the Web and turned on the *CNN* streaming video feed. Talking heads were talking about the impending presidential speech, in the strained enunciation that they usually enlist to add weight to the usual banalities. The president will put the short-term damage in the perspective of the long-term goal. He will be resonant. His speechwriters have been at it for weeks. He edited it himself yesterday, punched up some key points, made it more hard-hitting. Tight security in New York, the New Yorkers angry. He will make an overture to the French. No, he will let the French go screw themselves; he will make an overture to the Germans.

And then, at the stroke of the hour, the president appeared and started saying the things that presidents must say. They had been predicted accurately by the talking heads only because they had been said a thousand times before. Necessary sacrifices; greater good; prayer.

But it did not matter. Behind him stood the horse, the bull, the screaming mother, the light bulb sun. The silent heavenward wails drowned out the president's words. It was like a pop concert where the greatest band in the world makes a surprise appearance to play backup for the singer of the moment. Suddenly, the crowds have eyes and ears only for the band, and the song's words become inaudible.

But the performer and the famous backdrop behind him did not strike any harmonious chords in this case. The unspeakable horror on the faces had taken the speech over by force. The charismatic speaker, his eloquent speechwriters, the state with all its paraphernalia, were powerless to explain it away. I thought I could see drops of sweat forming on the president's brow, as if from the heat of the *Guernica* sun.

So TJ had done it, the little act of atonement that I had requested from her before leaving her office. I imagined her using her vaunted powers of persuasion with her spy-masters, whoever they might be, for one more time. Explosive kiss-and-tell letter in the wrong hands, she would have told them. Bitter but acceptable price to pay to avoid embarrassment, scandal, worse. The system must oblige to survive.

I looked past the president, now sweating profusely, at the left panel. The mother was frozen in time holding her little baby. It was the mother whose recent embodiment TJ had seen on *CNN*, or *Al Jazeera*. She could be Iraqi, or American. She could be TJ's own mother, or her own missed motherhood. Pablo, like Marcel, was universal.

I had very mixed success in this project. I had proven rather incompetent as a researcher, with a knack for discovering what was spoon-fed to me. But I had succeeded in one thing. I had disproved conclusively the sailor portraitist's witticism, on both counts. Art was revolutionary. And the police were powerless to stop it.

CHAPTER 22

▼

Or so I thought at the time. It was November 20, 2004, more than a year after the president's UN press conference. I was in my office, browsing the Web. X was the subject of a small piece in the Style section of the *Post*, elevated by the Internet layout to a status equal with that of any earth-shattering story. He had been appointed chair of a newly-minted Art Protection Commission.

I had heard the news the day before, from Nolan. He had chuckled about what he explained was an unfortunate choice of name. A notorious Art Protection Commission had operated in Rome during the Second World War. It had misplaced a number of crates that contained, among other masterpieces, Brueghel's "*The Blind Leading the Blind.*" The crates miraculously showed up at Göring's cottage near Berlin.

It was nevertheless a plum appointment. Also sitting on the commission were many high-powered names of the art world. X had evidently attained the position he had craved—Zeus among the art-collecting Olympians. Aided by what limited expertise I had gained thanks to my work on his project, I had myself taken my first humble steps into the world of collecting. Ever the conservative lawyer, of course, I was extra-careful to avoid the pitfalls that novice collectors often stumble into.

Nolan, for his part, had also been appointed to a prestigious body. The Vatican had improbably invited him to join the Committee for the Restoration of the Defender of the Faith. It was another unhappy choice of name, as its English acronym, COREDEF, evoked a state of military alert. He certainly had a strange love-hate relationship with the seat of the catholic church's authority.

Sadly, I had also lost Paul. The death of an uncle had taken him abroad for a week. Upon returning, he announced he had decided to pursue a doctoral thesis on art and propaganda in Switzerland. Even though he didn't say it, I knew the real reason for his departure. The pedestrian projects that are the bread-and-butter of our practice were no match for the excitement of our one-week foray into the war of art. I would miss him. Aside from his brilliant work on this and other matters, a genuine fondness and mutual respect had developed between us.

The president had won the election. With their usual manic waste of energy, the talking heads had launched another of their cacophonous exercises. They had set out to develop a consensus about the reasons for his victory.

For all the appearance of chaos, these endeavors are governed by rigid rules. First of all, every victory must be analyzed as the other guy's defeat. The sadism of enjoying somebody's fall is a crucial element of any entertainment. To be fair, broadcast news shares this trait with Greek tragedy (hubris brings down the perfect hero), and with the Roman version of lion-taming at the Colosseum.

The process continues with the arbitrary choice of a tiny fact. Say, the challenger was too manly, or not manly enough, when engaging in one of his would-be presidential sports. Having picked your fact, you then try to parlay it into truth by shouting over the proponents of other, equally arbitrary theories.

Soon one view will prevail—the more whimsical, the better its chances. The common ground of an idiotic harmony will be found. Each talking head will now claim credit for uncovering the link between the winning tiny fact and the loss of the presidency. And finally, in a self-fulfilling prophecy, that link will take on the patina of lore and receive the rubber stamp of history. One candidate lost because he perspired. Another, because he did not shave twice. Another was not angry enough at the prospect of his wife's rape and murder. If newspapers are the first draft of history, the last draft is neither more polished, nor more accurate.

So it came to happen with this challenger's failure. The initial explanations were many. His sports were too patrician. His gait was too swaggering. His smirk set his mouth at too steep an angle with the rest of his face. The pundits screened the debates frame by frame for any evidence of nervous tics or liquid secretions that could account for his defeat.

But in the end, the pundits settled on an explanation that seemed too quirky even by these standards. The challenger lost because he had won. He had outperformed the president in the debates. His eloquence had outshone the president so much that it had elicited the audience's sporting fair play—sympathy for the underdog. The debates had worked like a Wimbledon final where the applause is reserved for the obscure black girl doing battle against the number one seed. In these circumstances, the president's inarticulate bluntness became more an asset than a liability. Under such a barrage of words, the president's silent gifts stood out more easily. His empathy, his magic talent for clicking with the American voter, had the field to themselves.

The president had thus won on the criterion that, according to the pundits, most voters apply. Who would you rather have a barbecue with? The nice guy or the articulate guy? Who would you sit next to on the airplane? This last question is associated with the talking heads' propensity to lecture co-passengers in that cauldron of inane conversation, the first-class cabin. Would you rather sit with the silent guy who will listen, or the flimflammer who will talk back? The challenger's brilliant performance at the debates had made the choice easy—the other guy.

For once, the pundits had it about right. Schooled by TJ, I understood what they were saying. Words don't count any more. Persuasion is dead. Only the convinced can be convinced. Conviction is the result of images, not words. And the president's PR men had endowed him with images galore. The sturdy pillar of strength in times of danger. The strong, silent type. The man to keep us safe from the pack of wolves roaming the countryside in one of the president's ads. The busy man who takes the time to read scripture every day "to be in the word." This was a word instilled subliminally in millions, but never spoken.

Not that the challenger had not played the same game. He had. It was just that the images conjured up by *his* PR army were more obvious, less evocative. They were less artful.

But something else troubled me. The president's victory also meant that he had survived unscathed his own silent debate—with *Guernica*. In the end, the tears and screams had counted for nothing. Pablo's great art had been eclipsed by the art of the president's propagandists. Art was not revolutionary any longer. The police had stopped it. TJ had appropriated the power of its images for the benefit of her masters.

How would Pablo have taken his defeat? With fury, I was sure. Pablo was a competitive man. All his life he had competed. With Braque, with Matisse. He had always come out ahead. Until he lost to a pamphleteer. He lost to TJ. Imagine the world's greatest marathon man visiting his local gym. He is out-endured by the man running on the treadmill next to him. After three excruciating hours, he turns to have a look at his rival. It is, in fact, a woman with a flat stomach, running on without breaking a sweat.

Marcel would have been more philosophical about it. If you have discovered futility, would you be surprised if the discovery itself proved futile? For Marcel, the only paradise was a paradise lost. So what if his art had failed to change the course of history? Improvement was a foreign word in his lexicon. He might have been a little melancholy, it is true, to discover one thing. Of all his rivers of mellifluous words, the relic of his unhappy life that came closest to affecting the world consisted of a few sentences that he had not written. It was Andrée's love note. Scribbled on the back of an official memo.

And what about TJ? Would she greet her triumph with a sense of vindication or with her newfound emotion of remorse? I would never know. TJ had passed away two days before. She had fallen off her horse. According to Nolan, her beautiful face was mangled unrecognizably by an iron bar that was in the way of her fall. "Former Equestrian Meets Unlikely Death," read the *New York Times* obituary on my computer screen. With unwitting irony, the reporter described her as "a noted patron of the arts." No age was given. Like Andrée, she was leaving no known survivors.

I did owe her an epitaph. A brief one, just two words. I wrote "please shred" across Andrée's love note and placed it in the Out box.

MEMORANDUM

TO: Philip Melanchthon
FROM: Paul J.G. Rhinelander
RE: Facts and Fiction in *The War of Art*

At your request, this memorandum sets forth the results of my preliminary research about the factual assertions made in a manuscript document entitled *The War of Art*. You have explained to me that the manuscript is "a work of historical fiction," and that I should bill my time on this matter to your business development account. You have asked me to separate facts from fiction and to verify all statements of fact in the manuscript.

I need to start with some important qualifications. First caveat: the manuscript is rife with references to a character called "Paul." Paul is described as an associate working for the story's narrator and hero, whose name is given only as "Mr. Melanchthon." Paul's face has the shape of a rhombus, but his features "border on the cherubic." He sometimes displays flashes of impatience but quickly suppresses them. The narrator also offers numerous surmises about Paul's state of mind. Paul is thrilled at the unorthodox project that he has been assigned. A "mutual fondness and respect" develops between the narrator and Paul. When Paul eventually leaves the firm, the narrator knows the real reason: "The pedestrian projects that are the bread-and-butter of our practice were no match for the excitement of our one-week foray into the war of art." This memorandum will not comment on any of these matters.

Second caveat: As I have discussed with you repeatedly, this memorandum is necessarily limited by the unorthodox nature of the assignment. The gleaning and verification of facts from a work of "historical fiction" have nothing to do with the practice of law. As I have told you, neither my schooling nor my training qualifies me for tasks of this nature. I have repeatedly made to you requests for normal billable projects. These requests have been either gruffly dismissed or totally ignored. Under separate cover, I am sending by inter-office mail a notice of my decision to leave the firm, effective immediately.

Subject to these qualifications, my tentative conclusion is that the task you have set is almost impossible. Virtually every single assertion that purports to be factual in the manuscript is infected with fantasy. While the dosage is different in each case, it makes the job of separating fact from fiction extremely difficult to say the least. In these circumstances, it is hard to know even where to begin. I will start by listing the handful of statements in the manuscript that appear true beyond dispute. I will continue with those statements that have a progressively increasing element of fantasy. And I will conclude with a few examples of the assertions that unhappily make up the vast majority of the work—those made out of whole cloth.

The Few Truths

Picasso painted *Guernica*. He drew anti-Franco cartoons. He pasted at least one newspaper war story in a collage. He sculpted at least one cigar from wood, but I have no idea if it qualifies as a Churchill. He liked women. He often portrayed them in a distorted manner, often unflatteringly. He had a cubist and a classicist style, among others. He stayed at the Savoy in London at least once. He was a member of the French communist party, at least at one time.

Guernica was vandalized while at the Modern in New York. The city is called Gernika in Basque. At least one right-wing historian has argued that the bombing was a minor incident, and that it was used opportunistically by Picasso.

The *Guernica* tapestry was hidden for a press conference given by the secretary of state at the United Nations in 2003. The press conference was on the subject of Iraq. A *New York Times* columnist did comment on the incident.

Marcel Proust was French. He did write *In Search of Lost Time*. Albertine and her friend Andrée are characters in that work. Albertine is a lesbian. She does die in a riding accident. The young narrator does witness a sadomasochistic scene between the daughter of the composer Vinteuil and her girlfriend.

Proust did attend the party of the Schiffs, as did Picasso and Joyce. He did have a pedestrian conversation with Joyce about the weather. The quotes from Painter's biography and from *La Recherche* itself are accurate. Proust is said to have enjoyed the torture of rats. Painter does state that rats are a frequent homosexual fixation, but does not offer any authority.

Vladimir Nabokov was Russian. He did write *Lolita* and *Ada*. The quoted passage from *Ada* is accurate.

Jacques-Emile Blanche did paint Proust's portrait.

Robert Rauschenberg did exhibit an erased De Kooning as his work.

Philip Guston did abandon abstract expressionism to paint figurative works in the 1970s. He did draw cartoons of President Nixon. He was greeted with condemnation from the modern art orthodoxy.

The Vatican did abolish the office of Advocatus Diaboli in the 1980s.

That is about it.

The Many Half-Truths

Proust did visit Cabourg many times, but the last visit that anyone chronicles was in August 1914, not 1916. Doubtless the earlier year did not fit well with the author's fictional timeline. Also, there is no hard evidence that whoever inspired Albertine's character was there in 1914. And there is absolutely no evidence that Picasso was there at any time.

There is a surviving photograph of a young Proust handling a tennis racket like a banjo. He is in the company of three young girls. Again, however, the manuscript misdates the photo, this time by decades, to suit the story's needs. What is worse, the distortion is deliberate. The author has the character Paul acknowledge the year given by Painter for the photo—1891. The fictional Paul offers the excuse that Painter was wrong. This excuse is frivolous—it has no basis whatsoever. A 1909 letter written by Proust is also postdated by some seven years for the sake of the same expediency.

A French scholar did write a book about how New York stole the idea of modern art from Paris. True to form, however, the author blatantly misdates the book by a couple of decades to make it fit in his timeline. It was published in the 1980s, not in the 1960s, as the manuscript implies.

An art work featuring an ant colony was indeed damaged at an art show in the 1990s. It is true that the ants were killed by the leaking formaldehyde from a nearby exhibit. But there is no evidence that the work belonged to anyone by the ludicrous name of X. The account of the ensuing litigation with an insurance company is likewise groundless.

Piero Manzoni did sell his excrement in jars. The name of the series is *Merda d' Artista*. It is true that the jars are somewhat inordinately prized. One was recently estimated by an auction house at twenty to twenty-five thousand euros. I could find no support, however, for the alleged dispute between a collector and her daughter over the mother's obsessive purchases of Manzoni jars.

Warhol and Serrano did work with urine. The idea of urine-based art was mentioned in Pasolini's film *Teorema* in the 1960s, before either artist was inspired to create his works. But the alleged use of semen on canvas appears to be a total fiction.

The Countless Untruths—A Few Examples

There is no record of an organization by the name of North America Research and Technology or NART, either in Tysons Corner or throughout the Greater Washington area.

There is likewise no record of a shady billionaire by the name of X.

Needless to say, there is no record of an Andrée Duplessis.

Nor is there any evidence of collaboration between the German propaganda ministry and a "maverick" special branch of the U.S. government in the 1930s, or at any time. The notion is ludicrous. Indeed, this particular fabrication exemplifies well the extent of the shameless license that the author has given himself. I have been able to locate a comment made by a hapless Boston art critic on the Nazi degenerate art show, held in Munich in 1937: "There are probably plenty of people—art lovers—in Boston who will side with Hitler in this particular purge." The author has evidently lifted this cretinous comment almost verbatim to make it part of the "smoking gun" memorandum.

Especially calumnious treatment is reserved for some of the well-known historical figures discussed in the manuscript. Joseph Goebbels is perhaps the best example. To read the story, Goebbels was the Third Reich's number one criminal mastermind. "Yoseph" did this, "Yoseph" did that. He "destroyed" art where he could. He "expropriated" it where he could not.

That version of events is far from the truth. Joseph Goebbels was thirty-five years old when Hitler appointed him Minister of Propaganda and Public Enlightenment. Most U.S. lawyers have not even been promoted from associate to partner at that age. He was a brilliant young man hampered by a clubfoot, snubbed by the aristocracy and the beautiful people. He was zealous. He made mistakes. And sure, he bears his part of the responsibility for the atrocious crimes perpetrated by the Nazis during those dark years—crimes against the Jewish people, the homosexuals, the conquered. The blood of tens of millions was on his hands too.

But he did not steal one pfennig. No record exists that he expropriated any art—Göring did that by the trainload. And there is certainly no proof that he destroyed any art.

The idea that he was either a demonic puppeteer or an omnipotent despot is also a fantasy. He seldom had Hitler's undivided attention. He endured countless evenings in the outlandish cold that Hitler imposed on his guests in his Obersalzberg villa, only to be upstaged by the lunacies of Borman. Many others ranked higher than him in the Third Reich, and had greater culpability. Göring, Himmler, Ribbentrop, Rosenberg: they all deserved to hang, both those who did hang and those who preempted it by suicide. But to paint Goebbels as the worst villain of all when the power-hungry Speer emerges as a redeemed sinner is a travesty. To depict him as the one and only architect of the Nazis' vast deception machine is libel pure and simple.

Most damning, the author has no time for compassion. He does not allow for man's capacity to atone for his sins, no matter how grave. Whatever the merits of the author's speculation about the unrecognizable body, he does not acknowledge the possibility that Dr. Paul Joseph Goebbels may have died a serene death.

One other protagonist of the work warrants comment—"TJ Moncrieff." She is without question the work's most artlessly rendered character. Her motives and actions, as well as the nexus between the two, are totally implausible. Psychologically, the narrator is in over his head deeper than with any other character. Perhaps most notably, the speculation about Ms. Moncrieff's sexuality and supposed barrenness is based almost exclusively on the narrator's dreams or frenetic imagination.

In unbearably purple prose, the narrator starts by "wondering" if TJ "had ever been mother to corporeal children." This is a cheap device to prepare the reader for the conclusion, later on in the manuscript, that TJ sees in *Guernica* "her own missed motherhood." There is no basis for this other than the narrator's capricious musings. The narrator also "imagines the fifty-something woman and the eighteen-year-old girl playing on the sand in Cabourg." Pathetically, he feels "jealousy mixed with arousal." As for the premonitory dream of Andrée and a young TJ that the narrator describes, it is too contrived a device to merit serious critique.

In the one instance where the narrator purports to rely on Ms. Moncrieff's own statements about a relationship with Andrée, the rendition rings almost certainly false. "And then the summer passed, and she left me. I don't remember in which order." A woman of Ms. Moncrieff's sophistication would have died before uttering such banalities.

In short, the author evidently believes that the label "historical fiction" gives him license to suck the blood of real men and women who lived and breathed—some of whom may still be alive. He besmirches reputations and plunders graves, all for the sake of a vainglorious story about art. *The*

War of Art gets an F, for Fake. It should meet the same fate as Andrée's love note.

P.J.G. II
666 Rue des Invalides
St. Sulpice
VD Suisse

My sweet baby

Hook, line, and sinker. *Monsieur l' Avocat* finally bought *La Clepsydre*. X somehow able to procure certificate of authenticity from Picasso estate. X has now repaid his debt. *L' Avocat* did not ask one question about where-abouts of picture in the 40s. He had to close on second mortgage and home equity. $6.5 m. Wired to Vatican account. Nolan will send you paperwork. Snakeman has disposed of A. Finally behind me, for good.

Still suffering about poor Papa. What matters is that he was serene in the end. You must carry the torch now. My baby, how I hope your foot is not bothering you too much. When you receive this, I will be flying to Buenos Aires. I can't wait to hold you in my arms,

Everlasting love

Maman

P.S. Always remember: the only paradise is a paradise won.

From *The New York Herald*
Page 7

December 20, 2004

Tongues are wagging all over New York about the disappearance of stunning supermodel Albertine Duplessis. Albertine, who has graced many of the city's billboards, has been missing for a month. New York parties and nightclubs have had to make do without their most shining star. On the bright side, analysts say that noticeably fewer hearts of New Yorkers have been broken during the past month. Friends are at a loss to explain her absence. She was last seen before heading for a riding weekend in Virginia. This is bizarre in itself, says a friend. Even though her French grandmother had been a noted equestrian in her time, Albertine was known to detest horses. But others are more sanguine. "The most likely culprit is her complicated love life," scoffed one. "She's nowhere to be found in Tribeca. So try her in Gomorrah."

978-0-595-36372-8
0-595-36372-5

12933476R00085

Made in the USA
Lexington, KY
05 January 2012